Draconis

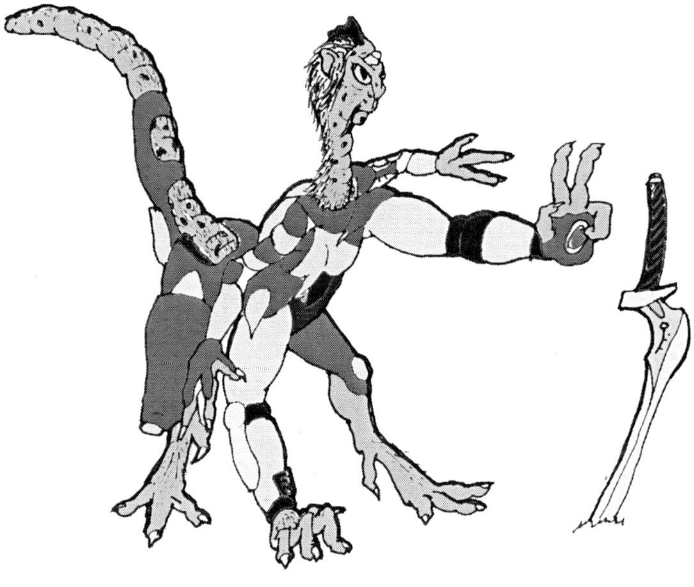

The Elder Stones

by Duane E. Naulls

RoseDog Books
PITTSBURGH, PENNSYLVANIA 15222

ISBN: 978-1-4349-9810-1
eISBN: 978-1-4349-5197-7
Printed in the United States of America

First Printing

For more information or to order additional books,
please contact:
RoseDog Books
701 Smithfield Street
Pittsburgh, Pennsylvania 15222
U.S.A.
1-800-834-1803
www.rosedogbookstore.com

Special Thanks:

Mrs. Lake, who opened up my talent

Harry E. Wannamaker, my grandfather and mentor

My parents, for all the encouragement they threw at me

The Nervous Wreck

Damon's mom called from the stairs. "We'll be home around Ten tonight."

"All right, Mom," Damon answered wearily. He didn't bother to inform them of the storm warning flashing on his computer screen.

The sound of the main entrance slamming shut triggered his impulsive drive. He immediately shut down the web browser and pulled up his Steam account. A few clicks later, he found himself cruising through the Arctic Wasteland with a crowbar in his hand.

Damon thought to whistle an old Dwarven tune here, but his gut told him to crank up some *Seven Inch Swine* instead. Ignoring the phone, he paused the game and set the satellite radio dial for *The Baron's Cove*. Back up the stairs Damon went, once again ignoring the phone. He couldn't speak one word now without spitting some sort of insult.

At least Zack wasn't there to taunt him at the stairs. Who'd know how much of a mess that little twerp would make with a bloody nose?

Damon smirked. He was not going there. Not then. Not ever.

He raced up the stairs to his game. Play now. Read later.

Later happened the moment Damon reached his desk chair. Off he went to his shelf of Manga and sci-fi books. *Golden Owl Tree...Shinobi Punk...Saurian Explorer*...Ah!

Damon slid out the autographed copy of *Werewolf Patrol*, not exactly the type of comic a thirteen-going-on-fourteen-year old should be reading according to Mom. Damon never cared for the powers that be. Lately, they've become blind to their second son aiming fastballs at Damon's face.

Zack.

Dumb, stupid Zack.

Damon slumped on his bed. The scratches of willow branches against his window directed him to a pair of owl eyes. He paused a moment, double taking the odd sight.

Owl eyes? He pondered. It could've been a barn owl. Those creepy things have broken from the forest across the highway every now and then.

A wailing howl jerked Damon out of bed. That dumb phone again! Couldn't the prankster call it a day for once?

Pause game. Stammer down the stairs. Pick up the phone and shout:

"Azeroth's not here, you idiot! Now shut up and leave me alone!"

Up the stairs again. Un-pause game and...

There went the phone again, right at the peak of a lightning flash from somewhere beyond his flimsy window. It always rattled whenever a big truck or a lightning storm passed by. That night, the storm felt like it'd reached the window's bane note. For all he knew, he'd have to deal with the broken glass and a soggy carpet the next morning.

The wail of the cordless phone didn't startle Damon that time. Mom always told him not to answer when it did that half ring she'd warn him about. He pictured himself like one of those cartoons turning into skeletons when they'd get smacked by Zeus' almighty bolt.

There was no way he was going to get his Mom mad again that night.

Still the phone rang.

Over and over again.

It would not stop.

Finally, Damon withdrew himself from the game, just as his Mute Man was about to be struck by an incoming brain crab. He stammered down the stairs, tripped and tumbled face first into the wooden floor. The phone taunted him at his carelessness. It still rang as he picked it up several stubby steps later.

"Be quick!" he exclaimed under a rattle of stress. "Weather's losing its' temper here."

No "Hello?" or "May I ask who's speaking?" this time. Damon had enough of formalities. He had been nice to everyone long enough.

Click!

The phone went dead the instant yet another flash lit up the back porch. The lights flickered. The subwoofer on Dad's high definition entertainment system bumped the hardwood floor, yet the darkness lasted hardly a heartbeat.

At least not yet.

Damon waited, phone in hand. He counted to ten and plopped the receiver back in its hub.

No ring. The jerk on the other line must've given up.

Good riddance.

He paced to the foot of the stairs, cursing every word for every step. A thought lingered, and he halted his progress half way. He turned back to the phone. Sure enough, the phone wailed in that one dying second. He waited for the power to cut out again, but the phone kept going. Damon threw his hands in the air.

The phone won by default.

"Hello?"

Okay, so Damon let his formality slip this one time. Maybe it wasn't the caller's fault this time.

"Do not hang up, if you please."

Damon blinked. He'd have hung up had the other side not spoken like a gentle giant.

"What?"

"Thank you," said the voice, still calm. "Now, if I could have your attention..."

Damon snapped. "For the last time, Azeroth is not here. And if you call again, I'll have Tracer Bullet come knocking on your door. Catch my drift?"

A short giggle raked Damon's ears. "Your mood shall get you nowhere, young sire."

"Spare me the formality."

Damon reached for the *End* button. A flash of light jerked his hand away. He could hear this creep at the other end, perhaps louder than the phone ought to let him.

"Hang up, and I shall be forced to..."

Damon never caught the rest of it. Another bolt of lightning crackled through the speaker. The dead tone rang fiercely in Damon's ear. He just shrugged and slapped the receiver back in the charger. He couldn't help but laugh.

The phone did its thing, as expected. Damon didn't bother listening to the other side's threat before barging in with his own demand.

"I'm not the one you're after," he boasted. "Okay, okay. What if I see this Azeroth guy, eh? What do you want me to tell him?"

"On the contrary," answered the caller. "I reserve my right to obtain the stone your grandfather had stolen from me.

Damon's heart felt like meat dipped in cold chicken stew. Since when did the stone thief knew his number?

"Two weeks!" Damon shot back. "See you in court, sucker!" He hit the *End* button and slammed the receiver in its charging dock.

What nerve!

More light flashed through the wobbly windows. Damon couldn't care less if he did see a fork of lightning over the neighbour's prized apple tree. Those potbellied pigs wouldn't dare come out anyway. What were their names again? Earl and Wilberforce?

Bah! Damon shook the bitter taste out of his mouth. He picked up the phone one last time. One call trace and a victory salmon and spring onions wrap later, it was over. The operator called. Damon suggested sending the police, then the phone clicked dead again. This time, the lights stayed out.

A drooping sigh overtook Damon's torso. He grabbed his Senators hockey mug of cola and fed his feet to the stairs. The thought of leaving the computer on in such turbulent weather is bad enough. At least the backup power brick under his desk kept his game saved.

Mute Man 3 awaited Damon's return. The screen blanked to a bone-crushing black in a matter of seconds. Damon cursed and gave note to himself: Never pause a game when an elite helicopter's laying the oppressive laws on you with its atomic missiles.

Damon shut the computer off. He left his mug and the flicker of his desk lamp. His closet called him for him. A lunch box waited behind the door flaps. He opened it for a peek.

Damon sighed with relief. Grandpa's stone never left its spot since the funeral.

The floorboard rattled to yet another cluster of thunder. Damon shut the closet door and the bedroom door tight. He made but one step back before reaching for the doorknob. His ears flickered at the sound of the lock clicking into place. The stone thief would have had to find another way in.

Damon turned away from the door. His baseball greeted his greasy fingers for the first time since he wondered into his parents' old room.

Was it really that long since he last played the minor leagues?

Four years?

Yes, that would sound right. That's when he had to smash something up for the sake of proving Dad wrong. What did he smash up? A gigantic egg stashed in Mom's secret compartment, bound to a nest of shredded flyers. Dad could never say it enough times, Damon remembered.

"I hate solicitation."

Whatever that meant.

A thunderclap rattled the windows. Damon jumped out of his shell. He crawled back to this senses the moment he regained first rights to his lungs. He allowed himself to sink into the scenery, into the long heart-pulsing darkness.

He stared at his bat, biting his lip in true fashion. Why must he be so jumpy? It wasn't like the thief was really going to jump out at him. No way! Not in the middle of a grand mall storm like this. Heck, even the old willow tree out of the window would have found cover if it could break free of its roots.

Damon slapped himself silly. He looked everywhere for something to distract him with, something that'd keep him from his window. That something came in the form of his magnet powered radio. He picked it up from the desk, slumped on his bed and wound the magnet crank.

Damon wound up his magnet-powered radio. He found the Emergency Broadcast System throughout a barrage of dead air.

"Funnel clouds reported in the area..."

Damon's heart froze. Tornadoes? This far east of Toronto? That's *insane!*

He set the radio aside, baseball bat in sight. He glared at it before shouting curses no mother could withstand.

The desk lamp flickered. Damon sighed. What next? The computer could never fix Damon's unsettled nerves, no matter how much of a distraction Mute Man 3 could become.

He grabbed a slab of paper and pencil at his desk. Maybe if he'd let his good hand draw him the shape of mind and logic, he could focus all these terrible memories out for good.

Damon bare drew one line when his head turned back to his closet. His lunch box taunted him with its stone cold silence. Its contents, a single ember stone and a blood stained pebble, were all that Damon could salvage from Grandpa's final journey.

Dismemberment

Damon's Grandpa prided himself with the ember stone. Damon couldn't remember a single moment when he noticed the stone in Grandpa's hand. Grandpa would always stroke it like some muted rock pet. And if the stone wasn't in his hands, it'd be in Grandpa's breast pocket, or tucked between his belt and pants.

Damon's Grandpa wouldn't let anyone else touch it. Damon couldn't care less. The stone never looked that cool anyway. It wouldn't sell for five cents at a yard auction. Not even the thief should have cared.

Yet the thief did, never realizing the impact it drove through the cottage one fine morning. Damon remembered it all too well.

It began with a loud bang, one loud enough to slap Damon out of his dream about fuzzy worms basking in a frying pan. The fact that these worms talked to him made no difference. It was only a dream, right?

Damon found himself shivering to the wind howling through the cracks of his poorly placed window. Or that could be the branches of the willow scratching against the distorted glass panes. Either way, the wind had picked up over the previous minute and a half. Damon groaned. Those funnel clouds had better not be real.

He eyed the progress on his paper. A sharply woven maze presented itself as an initial circle near the centre, branching itself out in such logical and creative patterns. Good, Damon sighed. *A good start*, he mustered to himself. This one proved his progressive excellence in line art like the many other drawings he started over these past two weeks. They speak out his innermost fears and his worst tempers without breaking that intimidating fourth wall.

He collected the memories he'd drawn out from thought, from the porch door of Grandpa's cottage slamming to Damon jumping into his water slippers at the heart of his chase. The fact that Damon had to hear a shotgun go off before he'd start chasing Grandpa into the bush...

And then came that most vital trip through upon gnarly roots sticking from the beaten soil. Damon had only his ears to follow Grandpa's progress through the family forest lot up to that point. He hadn't counted on the roots and teeth rocks obstructing his feet. He hadn't counted on discovering Grandpa's stone at that very spot.

Picking up the stone never crossed Damon's thoughts. He upped and scooped it from the earth on his way back to the chase. He remembered calling Grandpa's name enough times to count for maybe half the grandfathers in all of Ontario. Eventually, the real words broke out.

"Grandpa! Grandpa! Come back! I have your..."

Damon stumbled upon the cave in good time. He couldn't help but notice the distinguished features of the mining entrance. Who would miss all the rusted scrap metal lying around so close? And anyone sharp enough could see the wooden support beams sticking out of the cavern mouth a kilometer away.

Damon laughed. He finally found Zack's infamous hideout. Their Mom would have exploded on the little twerp the second she found out about this.

"They've been mining gold and uranium in these parts," Grandpa said whenever he'd reflect on his smoke pipe. "How long, you say? It depends on how angry the old spirits of the woods really are."

Damon didn't pay attention half the time. His nose kept distracting him with the smoke of Grandpa's pipe. And of course, Grandpa used to go on about how the miners dug too deep and opened up something that made them freak out and run away.

Too bad, Damon thought to himself. He clearly remembered reading about this in a classic fable about some invisibility ring and a place called Khaza Dung...or something that sounded like sewage waste anyway.

Damon stopped drawing for a moment. The circle had vanished now, having become an interlaced display of maze and Mayan-inspired line art. He could barely make out the stone that sent him to a hospital with a shattered leg and his Grandfather to an early grave. Its egg-like shape felt like the quartz he used to pick up around the lot back when he was Zack's age.

An ember of firm blue shone brilliant within the stone's center. Whereas Damon could barely hold the stone itself with one hand, he'd probably pick out the ember with a pinch of his thumb and middle finger.

That's how he remembered Grandpa's stone.

Damon thought to pick up the pack of pencil crayons stashed with his Manga comics, but steered away at the last minute. Colouring blue in his art would've probably ruined the texture and feel of it anyway.

He took a deep breath and raced back to the cave, or rather, tried to scramble out of it. A mindful gap in memory rested here. Damon couldn't remember how or why he ended up well inside this weird cave. Nor could he remember why Grandpa laid in a pool of his own blood. Whenever he thought of this gap, a great curtain of black stabbed him like a spoon to his throbbing temples.

What he did remember—and could never forget—was the horrendous roar of the cavern walls. Something had triggered a cave in.

Damon could never figure why he would be so stupid to race the crumbling rocks at the foot of the mouth. Yet he did.

And he made it with his left leg crushed beneath one of the boulders that stuck out from the rest. More boulders thought to push ahead, race this single boulder, and see how far they could really go. By the end of the rush, Damon's body had been covered. He had only his hand to reach out past the mess. Only his hand gave notice to any passerby that someone was trapped.

Of course, memory dragged him back into the darkness, and then onto a hospital bed woven of freshly baked sheets. Only his leg stood out, suspended above the covers, and encased in plaster. Minutes then hours passed before someone finally came in to check up on Damon. Then there was the doctor, and then half of his Mom's family.

Talk about embarrassing.

Damon blinked. The branches scratching his window snapped his nerves. He went to move, but the owl eyes stared him straight in the face. Damon winced.

Those eyes…they hadn't moved a single inch in this... Damon checked his battery clock…in the last half hour. Yet the old willow tree waved about like a vertical sea of weathered leaves—a beauty in its own sight. If Damon knew the slightest means of controlling his lines, he'd draw the willow tree that instant.

But those eyes...

Lightning barked in Damon's eyes. He wrenched his eyes back to the paper. A distraction would be well rewarding about now. Eyeing the pencil enough times seemed to do the trick. He rolled it into his fingers and readied himself for some more.

Damon figured himself lucky once, maybe many times before. But this one time, when he arose from the hospital bed with his leg in a cast, he had to blame someone else for this mess. The doctor said there were many fractures to heal, that the slightest pressure would send Damon's limp back in the stone ages, and yet, in a time of desperate attention to his bladder, he found himself scooting straight across the room to the toilet. He experienced not a single ounce of pain, not even on his trek back.

He figured it might have something to do with the adrenaline pulsing through his body. Yeah, body chemicals do that. They mask the pain away in desperate times. No wonder a barbarian or Spartan would chop a few more victims up before the fatal wound would finally get to them. But then, Damon was no brute warrior. He was only a natural at healing bad wounds well, like the time he cut himself deep while trying to cut a bagel. No one would notice a scar below his thumb. Not even Damon would think he'd cut himself with that meat cleaver so thick, and yet...

A jolt of light drew across his thoughts. He found his memories sticking to the one day his brain shattered—the funeral.

And what a funeral it was. It was full of perfume stink, full of miserable old goats and chatty soap fanatics. The odd man would stand out with ragged clothes and untamed beards. Damon could hardly remember the long list of relatives on Mom's side, close or distant. The fact that Grandma had three sisters and two brothers still living hardly accounted for the twelve first cousins Mom always related to.

And then it came; an onslaught of second and third cousins plus the relation-by-marriage factor.

Seesh! How could anyone cope with such a bother?

Damon sighed. Well, at least Dad was a loner.

Then there was Zack and their two cousins, Basil and Richard. They couldn't care less if they were at the swearing in of the new king of England (whoever that might be). Kids would always be kids, would always be brat. Like that last two (pointless) funerals, Zack somehow thought it'd be cool playing hide and seek with his bratty cousins. Of course, anything would be game (whatever that meant). Damon never had any doubts. Zack *did* think about hiding underneath the table where Grandpa's urn rested. The little brat would've easily hid in a nuclear exhaust pipe if Dad didn't stop him.

Oops! Zack got caught because his foot stuck way out from under the table cloth. BANG! *CRASH!* There went their Grandpa's urn, spilling what was left of the old-old man all over the rug. *SNAP!* went Mister Logic's strings. Then Damon jumped on him like a Budgett's frog ready to tear the little toad to shreds.

Damon didn't bother to recount the many shocked faces to come brushing down on him. He couldn't remember how foul his words were. Aside from Dad's iron grip on his arm, he remembered Zack's awkward speed all too well.

Not one—Damon emphasized this—not one of Damon's punches connected with Zack's face, no matter how hard or how fast he drove. All he could strike was dead air. "Stay still, you flipping toad!" he remembered repeating. "I'm teaching you a lesson here!"

Damon didn't bother speaking a single word when they got home. No matter how many times Dad tried to push logic in him and no matter how many times Mom tried to sympathize, Damon didn't bother to answer. He would have sooner chucked baseballs at Zack. Maybe one of them would actually break the toad's nose, maybe snap Zack out of his wicked manner.

Zack retaliated every single time. He'd catch these baseballs as if they were feathers and pin them right back at Damon. Each time, the balls would inch closer to the most sensitive anatomy a boy could have. Really! It was a test to see who'd get whacked out of their senses first.

Good thing Damon had mastered his reflexes. Good thing he had played every single game of pond hockey his friends could help him to. Good thing he had tested his reflexes on those smarter platform puzzle games where you'd basically mash the controller buttons to death or set up the right sequence of buttons to your quickest ability. Damon remembered beating "Ares' Revenge" twice—on the *God Mode* difficulty. No one else at school could do that, not even the game wizard in room One-Oh-Eight!

Zack never had the nerve or control to play these games, even if Dad were to allow him to play them. He never developed that hand-eye speed coordination Damon was so famous at. Dad used it as an excuse never to buy either of them a drum kit of any kind, even if one could use headphones.

But even if he could pull off a Guitar Master perfect combo in expert mode, Damon would rather try out the thinking man's crime thriller like that last one involving a dark knight and a violently sadistic clown.

Lightning crashed. Damon reordered his thoughts on the rattling window pane.

Weird. The owl eyes remained focused him.

Damon bit his lip. His drawing had somehow become a nerve-rattling display of curves and lines so complex, not even he could make sense of them. No longer did they read out a representation of his stone but more of a mind he never thought himself to have. The drawing called out to him almost as though it had a mind of its own.

Owl eyes!

He spun back to those demented eyes in the tree. More lightning crashed in the near distance. A figure formed from the darkness, one of the most absurd branches Damon had ever seen. All of them were branching from gnarly owl eyes so golden that one would think they were light bulbs.

A knot snared itself in Damon's gut. Something didn't feel right. The sound of these branches tapping on the window didn't place right in his ears. Yet, with the number of branches—at least four of them—there was no way to tell if this creature was any more than an owl.

Damon reached for his bat. A disembodied voice jerked him away.

"Leave it be!" The voice felt like pebbled gravy without the mashed potatoes.

"Leave me ALONE!" Damon belted, swiping his bat and aiming it at the window. "Leave me alone or I'll call the..."

The window exploded, cutting his words short. He cupped his arm over his face, too late to realize the mass of limbs upon him. He swung and he struck, but the mass overpowered him. The safety jerked away from his prying hands. Limb upon limb grappled his hands, then his shoulders. The weight of the attacker toppled him. A misstep threw him back, head first. Who knew hardwood floors could be so brutal?

He jerked one hand loose from the tangle of limbs. One good swing planted his fist with something squishy on the outside, stone hard on the inside. Damon didn't think a tree branch could do that.

Somehow, the assailant took hold of Damon's hand and slammed it back into the hardwood. How it could see in such minimal light like this was beyond Damon. Even owl eyes couldn't see that well in the dark.

The wondering mass spoke amidst a howl of wind and thunder. Damon's ears had clouded over amidst the rapid struggle. He let his anxiety embrace his heart, his breathing. The host of the seemingly minute owl eyes spoke once more.

"Where is the stone?"

Damon could hardly speak in such a groggy state. He tried to move, only to spot silver flash from behind the mass of multiple limbs. He felt something sharp upon the bridge of his throat.

The mass of limbs repeated itself.

"Where is the stone?"

Damon could not answer. He felt the pain pinch sharper into his throat.

"I ask again," said the mass of limbs. "Where is the stone you have taken from me?"

Damon dislodged his good hand then his left hand. One good punt into the nearest of many elbows embedded the assailant's dagger into the hardwood beneath Damon's ears. Another limb took over in an instant, wrapping what felt to be hammy fingers around Damon's throat. Damon dared not to move.

"I will not go as easy on you."

Those words rattled Damon's brain. He knew at once: the stone thief stood above, threatening him with brute and sharp strength.

"What does it matter?" Damon spat back. "You'll kill me anyway!"

The owl eyes blinked. "Your bloodline is too great for me to attempt such feat," answered the mass. "I asked of the stone politely from both you and your father. None will to sacrifice the deadly possession. Thus, I am forced to take the stone through means I have sworn not to practice."

The knot in Damon's stomach reefed at his gag reflex. Why did this guy have to talk like a medieval bishop?

"What about this Azeroth guy?" Damon pondered aloud.

Again, the owl eyes blinked. "He is your father, is he not?"

Damon stared. What the hell was that? Dad wasn't some guy named after a mythological place. Daniel Rodman Dmitri sounded more like it, though Damon could only remember seeing it once on an insurance form.

A thunderous force engulfed the room. It filled Damon's ears with such a booming nature as to rattle even his sight. A massive gap in the room filled the very spot where Damon's bed should have been. The spatter of rain filled his face. He no longer felt the weight of the assailant.

Baseboards cracked. Debris punctured the remaining walls. Lightning cracked everywhere. He blinked furiously, scanning the remnants of his room for both his baseball bat and the mass of limbs. Neither presented themselves within range of his weather-impaired senses.

Damon no longer found himself in the frying pan. He stood himself up, mindful of the floorboards so suddenly floppy. Every inch of movement resulted in the crunch and snapping of a collapsing structure. The house, once stable as a steel beam, had become undone by the very willow tree that saved his life.

He hugged the computer wall at once. The more support, the better. He shimmied his way to the one stable portion of the floor where the closet stuck out. That in mind, Damon swung leapt over the crackling floorboard, through the open door, and onto the lunch box. One swift swipe and a dash later, he found himself scooting down the longest hallway in the world. He made it down the stairs in record time, minding his feeble leg every third step.

A massive crashing noise stirred up his spine. Behind him, half the stairs vanished. Above him, a massive hole replaced much of the front wall. Damon didn't bother to see what on Earth would possibly crash through the house so easily. He bolted to the back stairs in a heartbeat.

Everything faltered around. Even that last damning step in the cellar snapped before Damon could finally seek retribution. Down he went, right on the cement floor. His lunch box broke apart at the hinges, spilling its contents in the midst of a hallowing scream. The stone rolled neatly beneath the oil tank.

Damon sprung to a spring, quickly spreading a reaching hand for the relic. Too late! Darkness instantly swallowed the stone and its soft blue ember. Damon dropped to his knees. In his mind, warnings of a tornado fast approaching flashed violently in blood red. Nevertheless, he couldn't leave the stone where it was.

More thunder rattled the house. The foundation cracked and groaned; warning signs of a structural collapse. Damon abandoned his retrieval in a fit of curses. To the abandoned icebox he went, makeshift shelter fast crossing his mind. He flipped the old freezer over its side, minding its massive ceramic hatch. A short push and heave later, he managed to wedge the freezer downside up between the narrowest portions of the cement foundation. With one last heave, he slid into the dank and musty confinements of the freezer and let it drop into place. Darkness followed.

In this darkness, Damon waited. He pictured the assailant scrambling through the battlefield that had become of his neighbourhood. He pictured the tornado swiping this assailant into its mouth, chewing it, and then spitting it out far into a cornfield.

Damon groaned pleasantly. Yeah, that would be so nice.

Mister Fuzzy

T*he Swamp Lizard.*

Damon couldn't help naming his prize mountain bike after some cheaply animated dune buggy. He tried every other name he could find, and still, the dumbest name of them all stuck like gum to the backside of a school desk.

It came as no surprise that Dad would call it babyish. But his Mom? Well, she couldn't care if Damon called his bike Mister Pinky, so long as it wasn't some sort of innuendo or something off a movie Dad would find offensive.

Dad didn't find half of the gory movies he had Damon watch offensive. In fact, Dad thought the ones with black men spitting four letter words every ten seconds were offensive. But what did that have to do with a mountain bike that made a rock garden feel like a stroll through the Don Valley Parking Lot?

Absolutely nothing.

Well, at least Grandma volunteered to lend the cottage for the time being. Everyone figured it'd be the new Dmitri home until the insurance landed them a house much closer to city limits. Soon, or Damon might face a new crowd and a new school up here, an hour and a bit full tilt from where home ought to be.

So, how did this morning start differently?

Damon woke up that morning counting the days since Mr. Owl Eyes broke through his window. He checked on his parents, neither of which showed sympathy for the tornado. Satisfied, Damon moved into the kitchen for a pair of salmon burrito wraps.

He buttered them with some 'mighty' caeser salad dressing, of course. No sort of whipped mayo could offer the quantity of omega-3's in this stuff.

Damon smirked. "Brain food!" he muttered silently. Mom didn't seem to notice. Her face was buried in banana bread.

So where was Zack of all things? Damon set himself at the breakfast bar between the sunken kitchen and the wondrous theatre room. He had half-expected Zack to jump out with a baseball to chuck at his mid section. By the time he panned through his list of web comics, Damon found himself stumped.

Really! Since when did Zack act so non-existent all of a sudden? He was such a mouthful the night before.

Damon panned to the left. The library study seemed its usual mahogany self. All the furniture seemed fit as always. The shelves of book were all in order, dusted, too. One of Grandma's ceramic ornaments somehow found its way into an otherwise empty fire pit. Other than that, there was no Zack in sight.

Damon turned right. All he got was the left stand-up speakers of Dad's entertainment system. He could go on about how the bass could blow up the house if one was to watch one of those heavily explosive Hollywood blockbusters. He could talk an ear of how crystal sharp the projection image shows up on the custom-sized black screen Dad had ordered from one of his home theatre distributors. (Dad was a home automation work guy of sorts.) He could go on about how one of Jimmy Page's lightning guitar solos could make a grown man's ears bleed. Yeah, he could go on about all that stuff, only to remind Dad that his oldest son still existed.

Nah!

So Damon hopped on his bike as usual. He couldn't care less how stressful the trails would be this late in the summer. That sort of physical stress couldn't even compare to the previous week.

He heard Mom call out for him. He didn't answer. He already strapped his helmet on and fed himself into his favourite trail.

Not five minutes into the trail of twists and tight grooves, Damon found his answer.

Zoe!

Damon skidded to a halt. Boy, did his disc brakes work well on these paths.

Zoe, Zack's one-on-one worker! That would explain that bit. Besides, didn't she drive the girly blue car next to Grandpa's old red-horn truck?

Thought after thought pulsed through Damon's head. How could that be? Zoe wasn't expected out here until around Nine Thirty-ish. Or did Damon forget to set his alarm clock again?

Blats!

Damon revved up his bike. A few quick pedals and he sped off at a hectic pace, through a tight cluster of trees, and then above and around a series of rock beds. Maybe he would be up a stiff hill and through a ridiculous rut. Ah, Damon couldn't remember what was where anymore. He had gone through this trail like half a billion times now, so everything felt the same as riding down a long a dull straight paved path. Maybe it had something to do with his multi-hundred dollar shocks.

Ah, such was the life of a mountain bike prospect. These past years, all Damon could think about were the twenty-four hour races Uncle Wilbur bragged about twice a year. Twenty-four hours of beating through brush and up torrential hill climbs! All in the name of getting the most amount of laps without breaking their bikes to kingdom come. Damon thought of training for these just to prove himself in front of Zack.

Hmph! As if Zack would've looked in his general direction.

A blotch of black struck Damon square in the eye. He swerved to the nearest tree and caught onto its lowest branches. That was better than an *endo* into the rocky surface here, even with his skateboard helmet on. He shivered in disgust, clawing at that miserable dragonfly wedged between his eyelids. It served him right for forgetting his bike shades.

He used a bit of water from his bike bottle to clear away a sting. The dragonfly, though dented, flew straight out of sight. Its lowly hum stirred Damon's thoughts. Why was he out here in the middle of the forest when there was all that sorting to do?

Maybe it was that absurd light that woke him up in the middle of the night. The night before, too.

And the night before that.

Leave it to Dad to turn Damon's favourite room into a computer study.

This whole past week since Dad fished Damon from the wreckage of the house Damon's nightmares worsened. There was more of that fuzzy worm in the frying pan stuff. Worse yet, every time the worm tried to speak, that silly light would turn on somewhere off in the boonies. It'd send Damon cursing at his front-side window, hissing and fuming at the spotlight hidden somewhere behind the mass canopy of oak and maple trees.

Sure, this tree housing Damon's bike was birch. Grandpa plated a bunch of odd trees about this forest. He did, after all, work as a lumberjack back in the days when writing left handed was still illegal in school.

It was not that a birch could act like a spotlight so late at night or would any other tree in this entire span of forest.

Thus, Damon remembered his one true goal this morning.

Damon found himself riding a gradual slope from the York Creek. He figured all it'd take to reach this so-called spotlight was to trek up the side of the creek from Grandpa's bridge about half a kilometer, then veer west up the sturdy hill.

Grandpa's lot, all two hundred and twelve acres of it, was set along the valley and riverbed of this great river flow. Damon found the river rather shallow for its width. Mostly everyone in the area called it a creek. Damon guessed it had to do with the riverbed being a mass layer of smoothed pebbles for kilometers at end.

An island rested here. No, actually, the river split itself around the base of a rather stubby mountain much like the one he checked out in Banff, only maybe a fifth of that magnitude. Regardless, the spotlight would have to be at the centre of this mountain, near its peak. How else could it shine so brilliantly from the cottage some five kilometers south and a little bit to the east?

Damon counted maybe thirty sets of fives with his pedals, with his gears at mid range. The grade here was a bit more on the gradual side of rough. With his legs so well toned in the last couple of riding weeks, Damon didn't find this to be much of a challenge, again because of these shocks. Then again, he hadn't expected a sudden rush of cottage orange fur to sideswipe his vision.

The screen went blank. Damon waited for the pulsing in his head to stop. Then he lifted his eyes lids as glaciers on a bed of water-drenched rock. His eyes blurred out the scenery for the moment, allowing him to focus on his body.

Sharp pain to the back. Blunt headache. Runny...bloody nose. Twisted ankle on one leg, throbbing agony on the other.

Yup. Someone had bushwhacked him. He figured it happened by either the largest squirrel known to mankind or a mass of limbs reeking of wet dog fur.

But why would Damon want to complain? The bloody nose healed itself rather quick. The ankle twist was really nothing. The sore back? Well, it wouldn't be much more than a pinky bruise tomorrow morning. The throbbing pain in the feeble leg could've been better, though.

In the wake of the cave-in, Damon had nursed his leg on his own time. Practically everyone hounded him left and right. "Don't walk on it!" Mom would say, like one of Dad's scratched up vinyl records. So would Grandma and half of Mom's side of the family that Damon actually remembered.

Not Dad.

In fact, Dad kept going on about how much a girly scout Damon "acted" on his first day back from the hospital, the day before the dreaded funeral.

"Suck that gut in!"

"Ow!"

"Quit that damn howling! You're making the junkyard hounds cry at the other end of town!"

"But Dad, it really..."

"Oh, shut up and play one of your stupid games! Those hounds won't hear you then."

Good old Dad, never caring about anyone's feelings. He looks for a hole in your soul and tore it to shred like a cat in a Santa costume.

At least these bones fixed themselves. Otherwise, Damon wouldn't be hopping his way back to Grandpa's bridge. Hell, he wouldn't have made it this far from the cottage had he followed the doctrine of broken legs. This leg should still be in the ceramic cast!

Funny, though, Damon couldn't help it. He couldn't decide which tickled his funny bone. Could a squirrel have ambushed him? It'd have to been the size of Texas to mess his bike up like that!

And there's no such thing.

Either way, not even Zack would believe this story.

Or maybe he would. After all, Zack kept talking about some Mister Fuzzy giving him kung fu or ninja lessons. "Ninjutsu!" Damon would correct at the earliest convenience. Then Dad would rip up his soul and scold him for being such a lousy "critic." Damon would have argued the difference between correcting a misstated fact and someone's lousy opinion, but that'd make Dad as grumpy as that tornado ripping through his house last week.

So who did Dad blame for that?

Supper came late that evening, partly due to the fact that Mom was worried sick.

Again.

Mom was always worried sick when family members would wonder out of her sight without telling her where they're heading. She almost always acted in the hippy-all-happy child-smothering paranoid personality Damon's school took her for. "That was an off day," he remembered using as an excuse every other day. Half the school didn't care. They'd laugh their heads off until Zack gets into the mess, fists swinging. Then the crowd would herd off and avoid both of them like the plague.

If only Damon could do the same with Dad's temper. Man, did he have it coming. The instant he stepped on the front porch, Dad belted every hate phrase he could muster, substituting every swear word with "lost!" or "weak!" Damon could march up to Dad's face and tell him to shut up. Again, the twenty-one inches of separation made him the shorter, inferior one.

Dad still had that coward streak in him, though. Not once had he struck anyone in or out of the family, not even the ones responsible for Zack's mentality collapse. That was and always would be Damon's job, so long that Zack didn't develop any true sense of spiritual independence.

The plates landed on the table one by one. Dad got first bite on the meal. Mom reminded him about mealtime prayers. Dad grumped about it but allowed the bowing of heads anyway. Zoe said the usual prayer, of course. Weird, though. Every time Damon looked at her, he'd thought her family would be more into the Chinese way of spirituality, with no god to look up to. Ah, it was only the Dharma thing of keeping one's mix of body, mind, and spirit all on the neutral side.

Or something like that.

Then dropped the question Damon had feared the most.

"Where's your dirt bike?"

Damon paused in the middle of chewing a slab of marinated pork. "Mountain bike, Mom," he said. He eyed Dad for a moment, but got nothing out of it.

Mom straightened her posture. "Well, they're the same thing, right?"

Damon opened his mouth first, but Zack beat him to the start line.

"Dirt bike's got motors in it. They fart poison all the time!"

Damon withheld the urge to laugh. Dad merely chuckled. Mom gave him the dirtiest possible look only a mother could muster. The laughter suffered instant death.

Their parents exchanged words about morals and Zack being a sponge of sorts. Damon ignored them. His meal of nuked potatoes and steamed vegetables called for him. No one mentioned any bikes thereafter.

Supper ended on a silent note. Even Zoe didn't speak as Damon helped her with the dishes. He stuck around the kitchen, drying each plate and utensil he touched, as well as the tea towel could let him. Mom did the washing part. Zack and Zoe were off finishing their evening routine. Dad sped off and did his own thing.

Zack burst into the kitchen somewhere in the middle. Damon caught a glimmer of silver in the runt's hands.

"Mom! Mom!" Zack exclaimed wildly. "Look what I..."

The silver flashed from Zack's hand straight into the ceiling. Damon felt the thud of Mom's feet rattle through his chest. Zack, on the other hand, stood perfectly still.

All eyes peered upon the object so oddly attracted to the ceiling. It looked like a ball but could very much have been an egg the way it punctured the ceiling. The exposed portion seemed to be scratched or marked with black crayon—Zack's doing, no doubt.

Mom gave Zack a stern eye. "What have I told you about walking into those mines?"

Zack gave his usual stutter and excuse about his imaginary friend giving the orb to him. "Mister Fuzzy told me to give it to Dad."

Damon shook his head. Zack snapped him a cold stare.

"What's your problem, jackass?"

Damon shrugged his shoulders. "Nothing, idiot." He returned to his tea towel and dishes.

Mom manhandled the matter from that point on. She swept Zack and Zoe onto the front porch before making her usual "Kids will be kids," she gasped. She swiped a bar stool on her beeline back to the kitchen.

Damon took two paces back. He didn't find any sense in standing underneath the projectile when Mom's coming at you like a herd of elephants. She slumped the bar stool right on cue, took two steps, and reached for the orb. Her hands slipped at each frantic tug. Damon imagined she'd be cursing under such a tight grip of teeth.

"Mom, I..."

Mom's arm slapped at the air. Her open palm faced Damon with a malicious vigor.

"Hand me the spoon."

Damon obeyed. He watched helplessly as Mom continued to prod at the stubborn orb left and right, up and down.

"Mom, I don't think..."

"Leave it to your father to hide his valuables under the bedroom floor."

Damon stole a glance. "Eh?"

Mom stopped altogether. Her spoon arm drooped to the side. That pair of menacing blue eyes beamed down upon Damon, blinking with perhaps as much vigor as her iron grip. Sometimes, Damon wondered if she was the one working out at the gym.

She handed him the spoon. "Meat cleaver."

Damon hesitated. "Mom, I..."

Mom dropped from the stool. "Forget it!" she scowled. "I'll get your father to fix this, and then he can tell me what the hell's he got stuffed up there." She blinked at Damon, as if to apologize for her cuss, but she simply looked away without saying another word. Damon ignored her mumbling for what it was worth.

Damon blinked. *Me, too*, he thought.

Damon finally reached the last of the dishes: the massive aluminum pot Mom uses to steam her vegetables. Damon hardly wrapped his towel hand around the handles when all nerves popped in his brain. Tickly fuzzy fur brushed across the bridge of his legs, right above his socks. His body seized in a rush of panic. That squirrel again!

He leapt back and chucked the pot at the intruder. A whip of drenched pain crossed his forearm.

"It's just a squirrel!" she snapped coldly.

"It tried to kill me!" Damon exclaimed. "Mom, I swear..."

Mom reached down with a subtle bow. She caught the squirrel by the base of the tail. Not once did she twitch or shriek. "See?" she explained as she showcased the noisy rodent. "The poor critter's probably lost its way."

She belted Zack's name like a foghorn. Damon winced. He stepped as far as the kitchen's constraints would allow him.

Zack called from the front porch. "Right here, Mom. You don't have to wail!"

"Manners!" Mom scolded as she escorted the squirrel beyond the front door. Her voice became muffles. A few quick minutes passed before Zack and Mom came in. Mom showcased the means of opening and shutting the screen door. Damon took the absence of the squirrel as a means to replace the pot from the dented floorboard.

It was the same screen door that alerted Damon to that fateful morning.

He winced every time the door slammed into place. Over and over, Mom revealed Captain Obvious to Major Sarcasm, the kid.

"Duh, Mom," Zack snapped back. "I've been opening and shutting door since..."

"Manners!" Mom snapped yet again. "Now I want you to open then close the door. Do this for five times. Then you will explain to me..."

Zack didn't wait for Mom to finish. He pushed the screen door wide open, stepped out, and slammed it back into place from behind. "ONE!" he shouted as he hooked onto the handle. He repeated the process.

SLAM!

"Two!"

Damon stomped his way up to the front door. One more time and Zack's going to wish he'd never been born.

SLAM! went the door. Damon didn't wait for Zack to count "Three." He gave the screen door his best shove. The force drew back straight into Zack's face. Back he went, tumbling and screaming all the way to the far lip of the front porch. He landed as a squealing mess of limbs over the cement step.

"CUT IT OUT!"

A dread of silence filled the air. Damon let the door slam against his face. He let all his rage steam from his nostrils. Every fiber in his body rattled with disgust. No one pebble of angst was left unturned.

In an instant, all of reality kicked him square in the face. What had Zack done to deserve this? He didn't kill Grandpa.

"Your room, please."

Damon blinked. Mom's voice hovered blindly in his right ear. He sensed both rage and shock from a voice so drenched with broken tears that it could only register as a whisper in the summer breeze.

Damon stepped back. He turned toward Mom. Air bubbles popped in his neck, grazing his nostrils with the tingle of hot blood.

"Mom, I..."

"Your room," Mom snapped boldly. "Now."

Damon bowed his head. He passed Mom to the stairs without saying a single word. He hadn't a single nerve left to apologize, not even to himself.

Damon slumped into his bedroom, silent as a distant bee. Before him, that same mess as before stared right in his face.

Sure, it might be a different bedroom, but it sure felt like the same mess.

No, not the clothes. They were all tucked into their designated drawers. The formal stuff was all hung up, and the insurance guys were even nice enough to hand over old copies of every single comic he owned. They even substituted his old junk computer for a state-of-the-art gaming power house. Was that cool, or what?

Damon settled for his desk, a pencil and some paper. He couldn't find the right mood to roam around a dystopian game field with brain crabs and helicopters that shoot out atomic bombs.

His first sketch landed him somewhere between an obelisk and some sort of walking lizard man with a snapping tail. The obelisk strummed a familiar tone, but could just as well have been something from a movie he's watched some time back.

Rap! Rap! Rap!

"H-YELL-oh!" Damon barked. He spun about, arms flailing like rubber bands. His heart buzzed aloud in his brain. Clenching a baseball bat at the ready immediately passed his thoughts.

The door crept open, slowly. Damon could recognize the fuzzy scar on Dad's hand any day. He sucked in his gut. Any second now, Hurricane Dmitri will hit land.

"Can I come in?"

Damon blinked. Dad seemed calm at the door. Not a trace of the demanding figure twitched in any way.

"Uh..." Damon hesitated. "I guess so." He turned to his bed. "I suppose I blew it, hunh?"

Dad took his seat at the computer desk. Damon couldn't help but groan at the unsightly mess of drawings scattered over the keyboard. Dad picked up one of the pieces. He prodded some of the lines with his finger. A curious gaze came upon his brow. Damon mimicked all too well.

"Dad?"

Dad smacked his lips. "I've seen these before, but I can't put a finger on it."

Damon simply stared. Dad returned the stare.

"Are you okay, Damon?"

Damon shook his head. "Well..." He scratched the back of his head. "No, not really. My temper's been a bit off since Grandpa was killed."

Dad nodded. "Understandable. I noticed that with your mother and myself as well."

He replaced the drawing and drew himself next to Damon. Damon felt the weight of his bed sag. Odd! Dad didn't look *that* heavy.

"Damon..." Dad drew a sigh as long as a winter breeze. "Damon, I know the stress you're under. It's happened to me before. However, you must understand. Zachary can't be your punching tool."

A shiver rattled Damon's heart. "Well, until I see Grandpa's killer again, Zack'll have to do."

"Worse things happened to people's ashes, you know."

Damon snorted. "Not deliberately, Dad." That was, for the most part, true.

A moment of silence staggered over the air. "Zack had no intention of knocking Grandpa's urn over, Damon. You know that, don't you?"

Damon bit his lip. "Just because Zack's autistic doesn't mean he does everything by accident. You have seen him act out rather strongly at Mom every now and then. You know, like with the screen door downstairs."

Dad nodded. "I didn't say that, Damon. In fact, Zack should have known better to treat your Mother so rudely."

Damon chose not to answer. *What of it, Dad?*

"Yes, what you did was wrong..." Dad's third sigh. "But again, Zack had no right to push your limits like that. Knowing how've you jumped at the screen door the last three days, it wouldn't have surprised me any if Zack meant to upset you."

A cheek rolled of laughter. Damon tilted his head Dad's way. "Well, I guess he bit more than he could chew."

"Chipped tooth," said Dad. "Maybe a little bit of a rash on his nose. Other than that, nothing serious."

Damon nodded. "Good."

"That's not what I wanted to talk about."

Damon sank his head low. "It's the squirrel thing, isn't it?" He noted Dad's deliberate nod. "Yeah, that kind of messed me up, too." Hesitation barked furiously throughout his cranium. "Dad, I think a squirrel tried to kill me back in the forest. Hung up my bike in pieces, too."

Dad looked puzzled. "A squirrel?"

"Yeah." Damon choked on his words. He felt Dad's arm wrap across the back of his shoulders.

"It's okay, son. It's only show and tell. Better to get it over with before the black consumes your heart."

Ah, The Dmitri's most prestigious quote. Dad must have said that a dozen times by now. Damon wondered how many times Mom would have heard such a wonderful quote.

But never on Zack. Zack would use some profane means of saying, "What's that supposed to mean, *hunh?*"

With a heave of godly breath, Damon dumped his confession on Dad's lap. He explained his matter with the spotlight and the monster squirrel.

Explaining stories was like deflating oneself like a helium balloon. Everything spilled out at once, no valve to trap any outgoing flow. That awful squeak would've sent Dad into a twitching fit. The more Damon spoke, the paler Dad's face turned. Something obviously got him spooked.

Damon didn't make a point of it. He let Dad slip out the door and into the wide open. Dumping a barrage of questions would only make Dad upset. Damon muted Zack's whines from outside by shutting his window. He opted to draw for a little while longer.

Origins

Damon's head finally hit the pillow at Two-oh-Seven in the morning. A familiar dream struck him as he shut his eyes.

In it, he stood in front of Dad's flat panel stove back home. Two of the heaters glared that full red. A frying pan occupied the third. Nothing else in the kitchen, not even the floating blob of water hovering over the sink, seemed out of place.

Damon stepped up to the frying pan. The fuzzy worm lifted his head from within, smiling as always. "Good morning to you," it said. Damon said nothing.

At this point, Damon expected everything else around him to go funky. He expected the ceiling to rain a shower of pots and pans. A baseball bat's supposed to shoot out of the sink and bat the floating blob of water into Damon's face. Then he was supposed to fall right into the frying pan and...

Wait a minute! Nothing happened!

Damon peeled his eyes away from the blob. The fuzzy worm demanded his attention.

"Look here," it said. "I have many a reputation, you know." Damon figured he had heard this voice somewhere before. The worm continued. "We must focus on the task at hand."

Damon tried to speak, but his mouth wouldn't move. He blinked as the fuzzy worm held out something from its fuzzy pockets. Damon leaned forth to find this object cradling in the worm's hand: a stone very much like Grandpa's, only with different markings. Still, the ember inside glowed a brilliant blue.

The worm held the stone high. "We must recover the remaining stones in the name of Azeroth."

All of reality struck Damon smack in the face. He reached out for the baseball bat in the sink, only to find a messed up knife. Damon drew his hand away. If he was going to kill the stone thief, he ought to use the bluntest tool he could find.

He made one swift move for the kitchen bar at the far end. The fuzzy worm, now nearly twice his size and full of limbs, blocked his most immediate access.

"I'd advise you to learn who your true enemy is first," said the worm. Damon caught sight of Grandpa's stone before the worm slammed it straight into his head.

Damon wailed and withered to a mass of galleries flashing before his eyes. Too many memories echoed through his head like disjointed voices searching for their lost souls. Grandpa's voice worked its way into the mix-mash somewhere, muttering about killer squirrels and broken family trees.

"Them deceives you!" One barked on. "All of you!"

Another voice said, "Your bloodline is cursed with my failures! Destroy the arcs! Make certain the Illori do not spread again."

Damon had enough. He shut his eyes and clenched his earlobes shut. "Shut up!" he howled in the midst of broken minds.

Then it came all silent, if only for one fateful moment. Damon took that moment to breathe out his anxiety. Anytime now, he would get that wakeup call he'd been waiting for.

The alarm clock buzzed at Seven Fifty in the morning. Damon rose from bed, stiff as a thigh bone. No doubt half his body was bruised from the squirrel attack.

He checked his computer desk, groggy as a hibernating bear. The sight upon him brought his senses to the tip of his fingers. Not a single inch of surface could be spotted beneath the layers upon layers of drawings.

Damon gasped. Now, how long had he been drawing? Four, maybe six hours? The alarm clock must've warned him somewhere.

He sorted through his drawings, sheet by sheet. The next one was in the exact same style as the last—every single one as complex line mazes. Yet each drawing presented itself as at least two different shapes. Damon recognized a lizard man, an Amazonian according to Zack. It held onto something like shotgun.

A simple shift or blink of the eyes and the Amazonian became a fountain. The fountain housed a great spire in the centre. Damon could see glyphs on this spire but simply couldn't interpret them.

He shifted to the first one.

Damon's Grandpa's stone. Damon recognized those glyphs all too well, and yet something tried to break out of these lines—a face, but of whom? Better yet, of what? The face resembled a Chinese monk bearing the resemblance of a nose-less cat. The whiskers brushed against Damon's fingertips as though they were alive.

A distant light flashed in Damon's head. The entire bedroom began to spin. His legs felt like jelly. He must be dehydrated. He immediately slouched his way to the stairs.

It took forever to reach the kitchen in such a great heap of fuzz. Damon's brain felt like crystallized salt. His heart fluttered as though it sucked on dry air. Every third step sent him into the side rail or the log wall. Managing past a clutter of oddball footwear did no better to his lost ego.

Damon finally reached the butcher block, striking its south-eastern corner with the padding of his gut. He groaned with a miserable bitterness in his mouth.

"Mom..."

Egad! Did he sound like a scratched up vinyl record or what?

Somewhere in this hassle of salty brains and blurry vision, he managed himself two guzzling mugs of water. The blur faded at the last gulp. The blast of cool moisture broke away that salty feeling like an avalanche of fresh arctic ice.

Damon tried his voice again. "Mom!" This time, his voice reached the high chords. He called for Mom one more time, hoping for an answer. None came.

A flap of yellow caught his eye. Upon the brim of the suspended potholder in front of him, a sticky note dangled loosely in the stiff wind. Damon blinked at this wind, spotting the screen door wide open. He leapt up, scanning at his feet for any hint of fuzz. The lack of squirrels brought ease to his breath. He resolved to shut the door.

A moment afterwards, Damon sat at the kitchen bar. In one hand, he had his first mug of orange juice. In the other, the sticky note glared at him with biting words.

Don't think I'd forget. Check the bike shop for your first chore.

Damon recognized Mom's writing in a snap. "Great," he hummed bitterly. He crumpled the note and chucked it in the fireplace. A quick note of err brought him to replace the note in its proper place: the burning box on the front porch. Then he made do with a salmon wrap for breakfast.

He made a beeline to the bike shop on the other side of the massive driveway. Hmph! *More like a parking lot for lost tourists*, Damon thought. He wondered how many times he'd have to turn around this time.

Where the heck did Mom go anyway?

A sigh rattled the back of Damon's teeth. Oh well. He might as well make the most of his punishment.

He chewed his last piece of breakfast as he slipped through the shop's main door. A deadly silence overtook him at once. Usually, there'd be Dad or Zack in here talking about bike or treasure hunting in the mines. Dad didn't usually share these stories with Mom.

"Obviously!" Damon sighed aloud.

The interior had been peppered with what first look like blocky stars of cream yellow. It became clear that the shop had been recently invaded by at least one slab of sticky notes in the preceding hours. Damon held back his laughter. It became clear Mom planned out the consequences for the day. Damon couldn't be any more surprised than a grizzly bear hibernating in the middle of a freak blizzard.

A quick peek from the shop window revealed the all too painful sight of Zoe's car. She was early, as always. It wasn't that hard to guess that Zack must've slipped out of bed and out of sight before either parent woke up. Their Mom wouldn't have called Zoe in this early otherwise.

Damon turned himself around. The gaggling sight of all those sticky notes drove the end of his optical nerves to the brink of insanity. He blinked his focus away from the bulk of the mess, only to find more along the tool shelf. He forced himself further away. Oh, where could the simplest task be?

Then he spotted the ugly woolsack in the middle of an otherwise empty work bench. Only one sticky note occupied this space. A meaty arrow pointed to the sack in person.

Damon peeled the sticky note from the bench. He had to blink several times to understand Dad's scratchy writing.

Damon.

Spotlight.

Damon crossed his brow. That was it? Two simple words? His name and a spotlight? His Dad had really got to learn how to assign consequences around here. His Mom would freak.

He set the sticky note aside. Damon couldn't be bothered staring at those other notes. In order of power in this family, Dad always came first, no matter the severity of Mom's tone. Even if Dad's chore looked like something tugged out of a junkyard car.

Wait!

Or did it come from the mines?

Damon brushed his index finger across the greasy fabric. The texture singed his flesh to a hot pink. He recognized the frailty of the old miner's sac all too easily. He licked the pain away. The taste swelled in his cheeks. He spat out the greasy residue. It reminded him when he licked his fingers after brushing them against the coals inside the family barbeque.

But something was added to this taste, like iron or something. Damon paused. It wasn't like Dad to start hunting for old relics in the mines. Zack would've fit the profile spot on.

Spotlight?

Maybe he'd check on that later. Dad would want whatever hid inside the sac washed up first. Given the amount of grease on this sack, Damon staggered over to the grease tub next to the main bench.

Boy, did this sac feel heavy. There would've been no way Zack could've carried this beast for an inch before he'd drop it on his toes. Damon jerked a laugh. Yeah, that'd make his day.

Mom laid a few sticky notes around the grease tub. Yeah, the water in there both stank and looked like the end of a dish-washing chore, but Mom only complained for her own wants. Dad had always said the water was too toxic to dump out in the forest. It seemed long due for an oil...err, water change.

Damon plopped the sac on the wash grate. The tub had its own water supply, however, recycling the wastewater with a high intensity spray. Damon minded to don Dad's bike apron first. He'd rather have his bleached red swimming trunks and mesh grey hoodie stain free for now. Oh, and the safety goggles ought to work for his eyes, too.

He worked the spray with a foot pump beneath the tub. The wooly texture tore apart like toilet paper in the middle of a monsoon. Damon set the hose away. He gave the torn fabric an odd stare. Wool shouldn't break up like that.

A box of rubber gloves caught his attention. He took a pair for his hands and peeled the fabric away. The remnants of wool tethered into the wastewater harmlessly. In its place, a massive grease ball hovered in Damon's hands.

He took the spray to the ball until all the grease had broken off. By then, Damon had smeared Dad's apron with the greasy sludge. He replaced the apron with a new one. Dad has plenty of them to spare.

Damon wrestled the slick object in his second pair of gloves. It looked like glass or quartz, and yet, it slipped out of these gloves like it were made of banana peels. He dropped the gloves in the waste bin and dried the object off. A hint of blue broke through the object's obscured surface.

Damon winced. That couldn't be right! It was Grandpa's stone!

Wait a sec! These markings didn't look right.

Damon gave a wandering glance through the lonely window behind the bench. Someone else must've found a matching pair, another one on this very lot where Grandpa had found his so long ago.

That would make Grandpa the thief, not his killer.

A spur of memories entangled with his frontal lobes. Of course! Grandpa could only go to that cave for one of two reasons. The stone thief was one. There must be more stones in that cave. But with the mouth completely collapsed, the stone thief couldn't have reached the other stones.

Maybe that was why the cave collapsed in the first place. The stone thief would have to make sure no one else snatches another one of these stones. He would have to account for all of them, including the one right here in Damon's hands.

Damon's heart sank to his knees. There was no way Grandpa's stone could be genuine now, no matter how unique these markings were.

So how many of these were there on this lot? How many of these did Grandpa know about? Could he have been the thief all this time? And Dad! How does he fit in this picture?

He couldn't! Damon bowed. Dad couldn't be a part of this mess. He simply couldn't.

Damon spun his thoughts about-faced. Dad kept quiet about his past life. He had no family as far as Mom was concerned. Dad never mentioned names. Dad never mentioned any family inheritance. He didn't show any family photos or drawings, either.

Damon shook his arms at his side. Why did he think all this for a stupid stone? Dad must have a reason to single this one out, of all things. Maybe he might know more about this mess than he's letting on.

Yes! Damon stood firm. He told his conscious there'd be no other way to finish this. Dad must help him finish this mess Grandpa started. All things must be set in their right place, especially this quartz stone.

Damon stuffed the stone in his backpack. He wondered for a moment of thought. Would Mom dare to yank Damon from this? Or would she protect him if the stone thief ever caught wind of Dad's movements?

There was no way to tell. Dad would have to know about Grandpa's stone. Damon must tell him everything. He snatched Dad's sticky note for reference.

Spotlight.

Dad wanted to meet him there with this stone. Yeah, that might pit Damon against that rabid squirrel. And then there was the stone thief, still waiting to snatch the stone from their grasp at any chance he took. It sounded too risky a task for Dad to hand down.

Still, Damon had to give it a shot. He still had to make up for Grandpa's mistakes.

He snatched the *Crappy Loaner* from the bike rack. Out the door and up the trails he pedaled. Damon couldn't turn back. Not even Mom would stop him.

The trail to Dad's so-called spotlight met Damon with a most curious display—squirrel fur scattered all up the hill from the river. It passed the tangle of bike parts and the wind chimes the *Swamp Lizard* had become. Damon ignored his bike. He ignored his mess behind him. He ignored all the urged screaming in the back of his head. He would not turn back. He was not a coward.

He made it to the apex of the hill in record time. Ha! Beat that, Lance Armstrong! The source of the spotlight should be over this next clutter of trees.

Damon parked the *Crappy Loaner* on the nearest cherry tree. A quick snack of energy bar suited his heart. He replaced the wrapper in his backpack, minded several sips from his water bottle, and then offered himself to the next cluster of trees.

"Ack!"

Stupid thorn brushes! Zack could bleed to death if he got lost in this mess.

Swat by swat, Damon pushed his way through the cheese grater of brushes. The stink of fresh greens tackled his nostrils. He held his breath. A good sneeze right now and he would poke his eyes out in this mess.

Light dawned on his face. At last, a clearing broke through the tangle of thorns and bitter smells. Damon shoved his might through the last of the cluster, parting it like a set of window curtains. The spotlight should be a few steps further.

He stepped lopsided into a clearing flatter than any of Dad's pancakes. The grass here hardly grew past the soles of Damon's air sneakers. It seemed too green, too evenly trimmed to be a part of the forest. Still, the brushes of thorns and vines scattered about the entire perimeter of this clearing all too well.

Damon winced. The fresh trickle of falling water drew his attention almost at once. A fountain stood erect in the dead center of a platform of well-cut stone. Whoever built the platform set it nearly perfectly in the center of the clearing. If that didn't smash the weird-oh meter, then the lack of any spotlight here certainly would.

Damon inched his way closer to this fountain. His eyes scanned every inch of this marble-crafted beauty for all it was worth. Yet, through this trouble, he could not find anything that would remotely resemble a spotlight.

He found the fountain itself to be a weird sight. Water streamed from but two pores upon a great spire in the center. Much of it ran through a crack on the southern end. The creek it formed ran back down the hill toward the river. Its bizarre hint of blue reminded Damon of his visit to the glacial lakes in western Alberta.

Damon made his way to the lip of the fountain. The water remained ankle deep within its cylindrical bowl. Any immediate glance and Damon would find nothing that would power this fountain. Nor did there seem to be any way the fountain could replenish itself so well. But then, Damon could very well have missed the hose and generator that would feed this fountain from the river. Any good would know that.

Well, maybe not Zack.

Thought aside, Damon rolled his sights upon the fountain's central spire. Three separate glyphs took the northern side of this triangular relic, each one its own individual character. Damon blinked. He had seen those glyphs before.

Shattered

"And good morning to you."

Damon leapt back. His knee bounced off the fountain's lip, shattering his focus like a glass bottle. He meant to shriek at this wonderfully crafted voice, but the pain got the best of him. Hopping back, Damon clenched his fist. Had he had his baseball bat, he'd always swung it at the stone thief.

The central figure of six limbs and a worm-like neck stood upon four limbs. The oddest metallic armour plating covered much of the creature's body suit. Damon couldn't decide if the plates were shells or chain mail. Fur stuck out at the joint of the joints upon his larger limbs. It stuck out all over his bodily chain mail and along the back of his elongated neck. Odd, though, there wasn't a hint of fur on his tail, also worm-like.

The smallest of limbs rested over what should have been the creature's front shoulders. Instead, an extra pair of shoulder housed these stubby limbs, albeit, with a shoulder cuff made of either gold or brass. Two flaps of fabric hung down either side of these mini arms. Behind them, a sturdy backpack rested on his horizontal back. It seemed stuffed well beyond its normal capacity.

Damon could see some Great Dane in this creature despite that cat-like face. The cockscomb and face horns didn't help determine the breed of some mix-and-match experiment.

"Hmph!" grunted the creature. "Mix and match is such a lowly insult from you."

Damon shivered. How could this creature speak so calmly? Did he even care what he did to Grandpa?

The creature lurched forward. Damon noticed a slight limp on its left hand...err, front leg. Seesh! Those paws look a lot more like monkey hands. He gazed upon Damon with those beady owl eyes. They glowed a feverish amber that not even the sunlight could diminish.

The creature's flesh must've been through a thousand summers of tanning the way the pigments worked over his many facial creases. This guy's got to be well past his prime.

"Don't you have anything to say?"

Again, Damon shivered. "Uh..." What could Damon say when he really needed his baseball bat?

The creature snorted, a grand smile inching on his left cheek. "I expected as much. No matter." He bowed his head with a slightly shut left eye. Did he blush or was that just heavy thinking? Damon couldn't tell.

Damon scanned the clearing again. Where was Dad?

"Is Azeroth to meet you here?"

The name sparked Damon's rage.

"AZEROTH IS NOT HERE!" he wailed.

"Quiet, fool!" hissed the creature. "The mercenaries might be using sonar devices here as well." The creature's eyes blinked a mile a minute. His limbs seemed slightly stressed.

"As if I care!" Damon blurted. "You keep asking about this Azeroth creep as if he's my Dad. And the way you look all mixed up, I take it he's an alien, too?"

The creature nodded. A smirk of doubt rolled off Damon's lips.

"He is your father, child." The creature stuck out its front left foot. "How can you not see this? How can you not see my words as the truth?"

Damon shivered with angst. "Did you just read my thoughts, you miserable...?"

The creature's eyes lit up. "I would be taking that, please." He pointed to Damon with one of his stubs. "In your backpack. You need not ask what I refer to."

Damon scowled. "You're not going near any of my stuff, punk!"

"That stone does not belong to you!" exclaimed the creature. "You cannot possess it at such a desperate hour."

"Oh, yes I can!" Damon howled. "Hey! Watch it! Get away from me!"

The creature advanced on his big four. Both stubs reached out as far as they could, inching closer and more rapidly with each step. Damon repented these steps. His brain swelled with uncertainty. He broke into a retreat toward the thorn brush. If only he could really outrun this freak of nature.

Limb upon limb rained down on him. The creature pummeled him face down and spread-eagled on the grass. Not one of his limbs was spared in the crossfire. The creature would still have two to work with.

What a freak, Damon thought.

Suddenly, the creature stirred, his face scrunched up like a rabid bulldog. "I am not a freak!" he reeled. "I am Lord Viggoti Fitzergauld the Fourteenth of the Altaic tribe. I am the last remaining elder of my people..."

"Like I care!" Damon wailed. Any jerk he made brought only misery to his shoulders and spine.

"Don't move!" warned the creature. "I merely ask for..."

A burst of blobby fireworks burst through the air. The creature's weight rolled off to the side. Droplets of cocoa-coloured ooze spattered before Damon's eyes. His ears thundered with a deafening silence only his heart could break. He could feel the thunder of heavy feet approach from the fountain.

The ground began to spin. A great tug grew over Damon's left arm. His world flipped itself over and back onto itself. Somewhere in the mess, Dad's voice called out for him.

"Good God! Are you okay?"

Odd. Dad hated religion.

The earth rattled like an earthquake. "Damon! Snap out of it!" Dad exclaimed somewhere. He didn't have to hold Damon's arms this tight.

Damon raised his hands. "I'm okay, Dad. Just let me have a breather, all right?"

Dad's hands slipped in release. His face looked beet red yet as dry as the Sahara. Obviously, Fitz's assault had stunned him. Damon couldn't help but notice the butt of Grandpa's old shotgun sticking from behind Dad's shoulders.

"I'm okay," Damon breathed at last. "Tell me what's going on..."

Dad's sweeping arm slashed the air from his lungs. He tumbled closer, closer to the fountain still. In the midst of the madness, he heard a feverish argument of fists and off-world sounds. A splash in the fountain brought Damon's attention to the icky blue water. The shotgun rested silently within.

"Damon, get out of here!" Dad bellowed somewhere in the tangle of limbs and fur. He seemed to have a decent handle on Fitz's surprising agility, and yet, he could never prevail against those stubs.

"Damon, run!"

Damon made up for lost air. He shot for the thorn brushes, only to tumble head first into the grass. Gnarly roots likely hid in the dirt feeding off the fountain overflow.

A mass of weight collapsed upon Damon's legs. He could feel Fitz's hammy hands dig for his backpack. "Give me that stone!" barked the creature, raving mad. "Give me that stone or I'll..."

A large swooping blur slammed into the mass of lead-weight limbs. Fitz's presence disappeared altogether. Damon blinked at the silence binding Dad's clumsy posture. Fitz somehow managed to tear a wide swath along Dad's chest. With what? Damon couldn't tell.

In this silence, Damon reached out for Dad. "What's going on?" he commanded. "What's your part in this?"

"You'll never understand!" Dad howled.

A blast of rock salt blasted through the air. Dad crumpled to his knees, his front side all bloodied. Damon's arm stung like a thousand steel whips had slashed through it. At least the punctures were superficial.

He grimaced slightly at the fountain. Fitz stood on his hind legs, the shotgun straddled gently in his front hands. A crater of blobby cocoa had formed on his left shoulder. Dad must have shot him there.

"That's because you never told him the truth!" said Fitz.

"He has no reason to know such pointless nonsense!" Dad hissed. "Damon deserves a normal life on this planet."

"You were to..." Fitz threw a gesture with his right arm. He gritted his teeth as if to bear tremendous pain."You were to convince foolish drunk to give up his stone. Now with it missing, we have no means of escaping the impending threat. The Buzzards would surely cut us down before..."

"He is my son!" Dad bellowed, "Not yours!"

"And how about Lord Zachary?" snuffed Fitz. "Have you forgotten of the linage you have agreed to? He is every bit my child as well."

"SHUT UP, YOU!"

Dad bolted for the mass of fur and silver. Fitz cocked the shotgun perhaps too hard. His entire right hand began to flop. Any attempt to recover was met with a full body tackle into the fountain. Damon pursued.

"Stop it!" he cried. "Stop fighting like babies!" He clawed at every inch of flesh and fabric he could reach. It was no use. One limb would slap him across the face. A second would grab him by the cuff of his shirt and pound him to the ground.

In the midst of all this grabbing and punching, Damon felt his hands wrap around something cool, something ribbed.

Dad's stone!

Damon lifted it over the mess. "I said stop it!" He barked. He took aim but found neither head to strike. Either one could prove as much disastrous.

A flash of silver ripped through the distilled air. Fitz had found the shotgun behind his back. Damon took aim and struck at the mechanical killer.

A heavenly light engulfed Damon's eyes. He felt his body lifted from the earth. Not a single trace of the clearing, high or low, could touch him. Somewhere in the bellowing of two baritone voices came a fiendish shriek. The pitch broke through, forcing Damon to clench his lobes shut. Yet he couldn't move his arms. In fact, his entire body had become limp in the gaze of this overpowering light.

Somewhere in the light, a voice cried in outright misery.

"He shall not be condemned to slavery..."

The voices cut right off.

Damon heard but saw nothing for what felt like forever. He felt high and low for any sign of grass. All he got was a tangle of sharp branches amidst a mass of thick air.

"...."

He called out names left and right without results. Even his insides couldn't hear what he had to say. *Impossible!* he thought. No amount of force could take that much sensory function out of him.

Damon called again and again. Someone answered, maybe Dad. But Dad wasn't calling out Damon's name.

"Dragon!" Damon thought Dad call. "Dragon! What have you...?"

Snap!

All of Damon's weight shoved him to the earth. A stinging sensation slapped across his back and shoulders. Ooh! Those thorn brushes again! He swatted the thorns away, one agonizing pass after another. He'd probably need a blood drive after all of this and maybe a new t-shirt.

He drew a sigh, a regrettable sigh. His body shivered faintly beneath the cover of his blurry vision. No matter how hard he blinked, this blur of heavenly light wouldn't go away.

Wait! He spotted some green over there.

And there! Tree barks.

Damon rubbed his eyes. His hands moistened with some sort of residue. It was not quite water, not quite oil either. Hmmm.... It smelt funny, too, like someone dabbed it in some wart of...

Bleagh!

Damon wished he hadn't wiped his mouth. What sort of substance was this? It tasted like....

Like....

Like monkey poop all smeared in with someone's leftover mashed potato. Or maybe that was the sort of thing that Fitz creature ate.

Damon slumped his way back to the clearing. He might as well wash this crap off at the fountain. There was no telling how poisonous it could be. One rinse cleared the blur from his eyes. The second made his mouth shrivel up in gasps of spit. Egad! This stuff was in the water for crying out loud! He glared at the fountain's spire. Where was the fountain getting its juice? What do those stupid glyphs mean?

A quiet moan yanked his sights from the spire. A slump of red and dark cloths rested at the clearing's lonely apple tree. Damon gasped.

"Dad!"

There could be no other. The Fitz guy's bolted for sure, likely with Dad's stone, too.

Damon took one step forth. His feeble leg crinkled like a bowl of rice cereal. He figured he would aggravate that bone sometime soon. He kept calling, kept hopping to Dad's tender body. No matter how hard his leg hurt, he had to reach out.

Finally, he slumped next to Dad's sluggish form. Damon could hardly look at him without shedding a tear. Much of Dad's vest had been torn away by the rock salt. His nose leaked crimson like a kitchen faucet. The pupils in his eyes didn't match.

Damon wept. Dad looked like an awful mess mess. His wounds seemed to broken for them to reach the cabin in time.

"Eh..."

Damon stirred. His eyes lit with a distant ray of hope. "Dad?" He wrapped his hands upon Dad's shoulders. Dad shifted to the left, grinding and groaning with each feeble breath. "Dad!" Damon exclaimed. "Dad, stay with me, please. Just for a little bit?"

Dad chuckled. "Dad? Who are you to call me someone who I am not, eh?"

Stings of grief raked Damon's insides. "Come on, Dad..." He reached for Dad's shoulder, but the broken man simply shoved him off.

"I have no son..." His breath wheezed worse than Damon's leg could crackle. "Damn, I can't even remember what year it is. What's your name, boy?"

Damon frowned. "Dad...Dad, it's me! Damon. Damon Dmitri. You're my Dad, right? Don't you remember? Daniel Dmitri?"

"I know who I am, boy!" Dad howled faintly. "I ain't that stupid. That beast who took my body on the other hand.... Oh, geesh! What did he do to my body? I don't think I can even lift my head out of this mess...."

Damon's mouth ran dry. What is Dad babbling about? Had he been hurt so bad that he could not recognize his own son? But he must, before...The man choked in laughter. "Ah, there it is," he smiled. "The beast who took my..." He grew suddenly silent, eyes rolling. Then in a menacing slump, he breathed no more. Damon reached out to touch him. His frigid hand trembled all the way to Dad's face. He had reached out too late. Dad's last words had all been wasted on a morbid illusion.

"Dad?" Damon sucked in his breath. "I'm sorry..."

"He is no father of yours, child!"

The sorrow seeped into Damon's pants. He wrenched his body around, eyes wider than a fridge door. A mass of green approached him with steps like Thor's thunder. This mass of green, nothing like the trees and the brushes, resembled that of the drawing Damon had seen only an hour ago.

The Amazonian lizard man stood before him, erect like any monstrous statue. Only, this guy was no statue. His tail swished to and fro behind his massive stance. His eyes, however tiny, drew nothing more than a petrified stare of pure ebony. Thorns stuck out his shoulder and spine. Clearly, this beast thrived off killing others.

At that very moment, this beast reached straight for Damon's throat!

Mom's Greatest Fear

Damon pedaled hard, much harder than he ought to. His feeble leg begged him to stop. It was on the verge of snapping again. He ignored it. He ignored all the pain in the world. He had to if he had to get Dad's body back home. Mom needed to listen. She needed to help even if it means seeing yet another member of the family dead in this past month.

Crap! Why did life have to be cruel? Why must it be so agonizing that not even death itself could touch Damon? How did he get to this?

A flash of the past five minutes barely registered in his brain. He barely remembered how the Amazonian suddenly looked far and away. He remembered the beast letting him go. "Tell your mother what has happened here," the beast said almost too human-like. Damon didn't hesitate to listen. He hadn't a trace of courage in his heart.

He barely made it to the tip of the driveway when Mom burst out of the cottage, baseball bat in hand. Damon didn't waste time explaining the situation, but Mom cut straight through him.

"Damon, I swear..."

Odd, Damon thought. Mom didn't usually swear unless some snarly beast jumped out at her. Something bugged her big time. Damon doubted the Amazonian had anything to do with it.

He reached out with his voice. "Mom! I...I need you to get the four-wheeler..."

"No time for that! In the house. Now!"

"But Mom..."

"I said, 'In the house,' Damon!"

She snatched him by the hand and dragged him to the house. He gave little resistance. She had broken through his resistance like a war tank filled to the brim with battering rams and the sort. She was well beyond his reasoning. What did it matter? At any rate, the Amazonian would likely sneak his way back here. Damon couldn't tell what an oversized grumpy Amazonian would do in the middle of a hot summer day.

He couldn't help but notice Zoe's car missing from the driveway. He hesitated to ask, even as Mom chucked him into the boot closet. He struck the back wall full tilt. All the winter jackets were stashed away about an hour's drive away.

"You stay in there!" Mom stated sternly. "I have no time for questions!"

Damon spun around, his face covered in sweat and blood. "But Mom..."

SLAM!

Too late! Darkness consumed the closet. Damon could hear the door rattle. The glacial paced sound of something massive dragging across the hardwood floor. He could hear faint mumbles and the occasional assurance of safety. Damon couldn't go for that. He'd rather have the truth about Dad.

The door rattled again. Damon burst into a sweat. He pushed at the door. It wouldn't budge an inch. He tried bunting it with his shoulders again and again. The door would not budge.

Whatever Mom put behind this door did the job Mom meant it for. Damon scanned the door with his hands. That stupid knot should be about chest level. He would be able to poke it out with a simple jab.

A flick of light stuck through the old hole. Damon heard the knot cork roll along the floorboards. A wave of silence followed. Good! Mom hadn't noticed. He pressed his knees against the door and took his precious peek.

Ugh! What an awful view. The back of the TV had been neglected for so long, not a single inch spared from dust bunnies. It obstructed his best angle inside this cramped space. He might never know what would come through the front door.

Mom, on the other hand, sat perfectly still at the bar. She faced her stool outward. She would have a good view of the driveway through Dad's massive sun-side window. She carried Grandpa's rifle in her hands. The way she shivered, it felt like she cradled a screaming baby to sleep.

Damon didn't bother to speak. He vowed not to breathe. No! That was a stupid vow. Don't breathe so hard on the door!

Suddenly, Mom's posture stiffened. She leapt out the stool, screaming "Go away!" The rifle rocked sharply in her hands. Damon could barely see her trigger finger wrap around the rifle's most lethal lever.

What was she doing? Damon gasped. She was bound to kill Zoe or Zack by mistake.

He pounded his fists against the door. "Mom! Stop!" he cried over. "Mom, please..." A harrowing shriek rattled his ears. The gun went off. Somewhere, glass shattered to the point of no return.

A swift swipe of green knocked the rifle straight to the knothole. Damon dropped to his feet in an abysmal rattle. He waited anxiously for the stench of urine to leave his pants.

No, wait! Maybe that was why the Amazonian let him go.

Yeah, that's it. It couldn't stand the smell of pee. Good, then! The Amazonian wouldn't even bother to....

Mom's shriek filled the air once more. A greater roar muted her scream in an instant. Damon didn't dare to peep through the knot hole no matter how many times the closet door rattled. No matter how much torture Mom stood through, Damon did not peep. His heart couldn't handle the stress.

Soon, only his heart would pound in his ears. Only the heat swelling on his face would burn his soul. The terrible violence upon his family would finally end. He would be the last man standing...kneeling. Not even Zack would survive.

Good riddance.

Damon let his heart cool. He rose from the stench of his urine. A quick peek through the knothole revealed but a field of shattered debris. The TV hand landed on its front somehow. It no longer blocked Damon's view from the front wall. He found only a massive gap where the front window should've been.

He pushed at the door. It cracked open with hardly an effort.

The air filled with the stench of rot, certainly not Damon's pants. His body rattled in the absences before him. Its abysmal stillness crept up Damon's back.

Minutes passed. Damon slipped out of his sneakers and into his clogs. The tangle of shards and splinters shouldn't be able to pass the sole.

"Mom?"

There was nothing, not even a peep, and not even a trace of blood.

In fact, the whole living space looked like a bomb had gone off. Books were shredded like coleslaw. Damon couldn't recognize a single shard of glass. All of Mom's sculptures had been smashed about like...like baby toys. Someone tore apart half the breakfast bar, likewise the Amazonian.

Damon gulped. He praised himself for running the opposite way from the beast's magnificent claws.

Again, he couldn't find a single trace of blood anywhere. It was like the Amazonian scooped Mom up and began trashing the place around. He might have picked up some sort of armour on his way over here, too. But then, the Amazonian never had that time to put any clothes on to begin with. He must have bled at least a little.

Yet, the great beast didn't shed a single drop. Damon's eyes never lied.

Wow, Damon thought. The great beast sure knew how to clean up after himself. Strange how he left everything else a disaster area, very much like Dad did with his bike shop every now and then.

Damon bit his lip. He couldn't help it. After all, she could have hid from that terrible beast. Damon pictured her hiding in the cupboard or maybe the old storage bin downstairs. Knowing how the Amazonian's nostrils would be ultra-sensitive, he wouldn't be able to get past that darn awful stink of moth-balls drenched in the cellar's condensation.

Arteries throbbed in his head. Life drained from the very memoirs of his family. He had no family left to care for. Even if Mom hid somewhere in the boonies, Damon wouldn't reach out for her. She had to have known about Dad's other personalities. She really had to. Even Zack would have had known. They all lied to Damon. It was his turn to return the trust fund.

They could wait—all of them. Damon had his own life to worry about now.

Damon whelped. His legs began to itch. No doubt, the urine made his legs raw. He might as well jump in a quick shower and be done with it.

He hopped up the stairs without further debate. He was not about to be caught dead with his pants soiled wet like this.

The shower did better than Damon had hoped for. In all his life, he'd never found the right time to stand in a gushing stream of steaming water for any longer than five seconds. The water bill had been so crazy in the city lately. Here, on the other hand, water came from a good hundred litre well. He couldn't possibly learn gallons to metric the way school worked these days.

More than enough time passed. Damon left the stall the instant his fingers felt like chalk salt. A slip into his combat pants and khaki shirt ought to work out for the moment. Maybe if he left his backpack by the door with a few things, he could be ready to hightail it out of sight the instant trouble knocked at what was left of the front door.

Damon searched the house high and low. He scanned every piece of the cellar, from the secret rifle stash to the meat locker. He couldn't find Mom anywhere.

Damon shrugged. Maybe she hid in the bike shop, better for him to sneak a few of her favourite cookies on his way out.

He reached the screen door when his stomach rumbled faintly. A salmon or chicken wrap felt like a decent fill-in. Damon slapped himself up a pair. He mulched down the first helping before settling at the breakfast bar. Not once did he see the phone.

"Where'd you stash it, Mom?"

No answer came. Damon didn't expect any from a ghost that didn't exist.

He reset his dishes carefully in the kitchen sink. At least the Amazonian didn't bother with the clutter in here.

Eh?

A flick of silver poked Damon in the eye. He followed the glare to the kitchen ceiling. Zack's metal ball still wedged itself in the stucco.

Damon glanced left to right. Now, after a whole night, why didn't any-one bother to unstuck the stupid ball? Was Zack that out of control that they couldn't even notice?

Oh, wait!

Damon smacked himself square in the face. How could they notice if the sun couldn't even shine on the dumb ball? Heh! He shrugged. Finders, keepers.

He repeated Mom's actions all at once. First, the last remaining bar stool slid prim and proper. Damon eyed the ball a few times to get the alignment right. He went on to fetch a stirring spoon. This ought to work better than whatever it was Mom used last night. With a great heave of air, he climbed the stool.

Mom would have had no problem jabbing the spoon in between the ball and the jip rock had the butcher's block been there. Count on a youthful stunt and Damon had no problem jabbing the spoon in place. Prying the sucker out of the ceiling, on the other hand, proved more than a workload for his shoulders. He could hardly keep his balance on the stool as it was.

Maybe one...more...shove...

SNAP!

A bluish liquid splashed in Damon's face. The stool vanished from Damon's feet. He tumbled amidst a thick gasp of air. His spoon hand throbbed with beating hearts. The handle had snapped off completely, but the ball remained the same.

Bleagh! This liquid tastes like toilet water! Damon whisked his favourite shirt fresh from the clean laundry of all things! He chucked the handle hard. "Stupid cheap metal!" he barked, kicking the busted stool out of the way.

He made his way up slowly, minding the puddle of blue all the way. He booted the rest of the bar stool from his person. The further he kept it out of sight, the better. He strummed his temples hard. Now what sort of sewage pipe did he bust now?

Damon made a mental note of the cottage blueprints. The kitchen was here, so shouldn't Mom and Dad's bedroom be right on top?

His face crumpled in distaste. That didn't make any sense! Damon's Grandpa didn't build any pipes under their bedroom or under any of the bedrooms for that matter. All the bathrooms were stacked one on top of each other at front and center, on the other side of the boot closet wall. The sewage made its way underneath the closet, right before Grandpa's secret stash of rifles. Dad never once complained of this setup. It was perhaps the most genius setup he had ever seen from Grandpa at any given time.

Damon had seen better, though. This kitchen ceiling was not that.

In fact, he'd yet to figure out why someone would offset the kitchen like this. Damon shook his head. This couldn't be right! No one in the right frame of mind would make the ceiling this offset, this low from the rest of the structure. There had to be something there. He had to be sure.

Yet when he checked the bedroom, he couldn't find anything that would indicate any sort of piping. The radiators peeked visibly from the walls. Damon couldn't sense anything remotely sewage or water related on this side of the room. Worse yet, Mom and Dad's bedroom took nearly a third more floor space than the kitchen would have.

This was wrong.

Damon glazed at his palms. Or was it?

After all, Dad had been keeping enough secrets as it was. He was really an Amazonian. He knew the stone thief all along. Hell! No wonder Dad didn't try to scold Zack over Mister Fuzzy, the imaginary friend. Mister Fuzzy was real!

Mister Fuzzy's hands were soaked in Grandpa's blood....

Damon shook his head. He shook really hard. The shower alone could not erase the day's drastic turn of events from his head. No amount of shower would do that. Hmph! If they were able to move the hot tub from their other house, it still wouldn't fix the issue. No, if anything, Damon needed the truth.

He was going to get to the truth once and for all.

He sucked in maybe a gallon of air and picked the corner furthest from the kingly bed. There, he tapped his heel lightly on the floor. The unmistakable emptiness beneath the floor sank into his heart.

Hollow.

He moved on a few spaces closer to the closet. *Tap! Tap!* Damon felt the hollowness ring beneath his feet and through his knuckles. A few steps more. *Tap! Tap!* Nope! Maybe another step here.

Thunk!

Damon stopped on the spot. He figured he stepped about six paces from the front wall. Here, the hollowness ended and the truth began.

He took two steps at an angle inward and tapped again.

Fancy Goggles

Damon covered the whole bedroom with his clogs. He shoved the furniture around in all sorts of angles. Indeed, this solid space grew in his mind. Still, he could not find the answer. The floorboard glistened with a brilliant gloss. He flipped all the mats he could find, only to boot at the air.

Where did Grandpa put the door?

He smacked his pal across his forehead. Oh, the closet, of course!

Damon threw the door open, only to be met with the most vile stench of mothballs he had come to face. His nose shriveled like a prune. Why did he have to be allergic to them?

One by one, he chucked boot after shoe after jacket out of the closet. He didn't bother with the shelves or the sides. The trap door should be at his feet. He could hear the lever calling his name.

Damon could not find any.

He dropped to his knees, fists pounding. "No!" he shouted. "No, no, no, no! No!"

KRAKK!

What? An explosion?

The air shifted weight around Damon's shoulder. Damon could never forget that whishing throb echoing in his ears. He figured the blast about a kilometer away, maybe a little more. How could he remember this sensitivity? It has haunted him ever since Zack lost his sanity.

He sighed with relief—first things first. He reached for the old baby cardboard box Mom had been using since who knew when. He could feel the bottle nipples as he gripped around the lip.

Click!

Damon jerked his hand away from the deepest corner. Merely a second ago, he knew Mom had stashed the nipples for Zack's baby bottles in this box. Now he knew. They weren't nipples. They were buttons.

He scattered around for a flashlight. One sharp aim spilt light upon a keypad perfectly hidden inside the box. But it wasn't a box. Damon couldn't move it an inch. He eyed the keypad some more.

A total of six buttons were laid upon a hexagon shape. Dead in center, a crystal glowed a green, reminding Damon of pea soup vomit. The outer buttons were littered with the oddest glyphs Damon had ever seen. Some of them looked like they were ripped right off some of his drawings. *No way!* Damon thought. Dad couldn't be stealing his ideas like that. This had to be a coincidence. He blinked with furor. Could it?

He pressed the crystal. Steam hissed in his armpits. The ground shivered like an earthquake, not as hard as Los Angeles yet not as soft as Oshawa. It shifted back before Damon could retreat. He fell head first into the wall, bouncing back with an utter groan. The trap door shuddered and shifted. Boots and shoes layered overhead collected like pieces of a magnetic puzzle. *No wonder Dad didn't wear any of them*, Damon thought.

He reached up, only to slip on what felt like the slickest silicon he'd ever felt. The trap door slammed hard in his face. Darkness swallowed his sights.

The earthquake jiggled his insides. That couldn't be right. There hasn't been an earthquake like this around here, ever. Damon knew there'd be too many rocks in the ground for such a violent shake.

Maybe it was a ship. Damon nodded. Yeah! It had got to be a ship. The Amazonian—Dad—would probably need a backup in case something happened. No wonder Grandpa wouldn't let Damon or Zack stumble away from any of the trails. Damon could have easily stumbled onto the ship, and when Damon saw something out of the picture, he didn't take a second chance to inspect it through and through.

Damon smirked. Grandpa was still right on that.

Then, his gut yanked on his heart. Darkness ebbed into a twilight blue. This little cubby hole of Dad emitted light like some sort of underwater cave. The walls, made of the clearest silicon, revealed a subtle system of LEDs littering the inner walls. They seemed pretty far in there, too. There must be—Damon figured at once—at least a foot of this blue liquid to cushion the insides. Damon blinked hard. The ceiling, too.

Damon sucked in his gut. *How cool can you get*? he thought. *Really, Dad! Why'd you have to keep these secrets?* Damon didn't find himself the show and tell type. Most of his school buddies did all of that for him since.... Who knows when? Kindergarten, maybe?

Anxiety pulsed everywhere. Its wobbly nature reminded Damon of Mom and Dad's bed perched just above his head. He had better cool it before he poked a hole in this stuff. A couple of *breather* cycles did the trick really nice.

He scanned the most immediate content to his right. Who knew Dad was so into old military ammo boxes and stuff? Who knew he collected movie props from some of the more recent Hollywood visits back at the military base? Some fancy wobble goggles here and a pulse rifle there.

Ha! This was so cool!

Blip!

What was that?

Damon froze chest first on the blobby floor. *Blip!* That sound! It came from the west... err, left! *Blip!* What the...? The metal ball rolled across the blobby surface like a pinball. How did that get there? Crap! Where was the leak?

Damon's hair stood on end. Damon rolled his palms across the floor. Where was the leak? He had to find it before the whole room began to flood on him! Where was the leak? Oh, where could he feel the water in a place like this? Why wasn't there any water to begin with? No sort of material could heal by itself.

Not on this planet, anyway.

Damon stopped in his tracks. Ha! Maybe this stuff wasn't from this planet to begin with. Maybe these goggles and this pulse rifle.... *Crap!* He wobbled his way to the back. He better not go near the gun then. Damon couldn't see how such a piece of alien warfare item could discharge in a cramped room like this. He opted for the metal ball instead and maybe the goggles.

Damon tried the goggles on. They slipped perfectly behind Damon's ears like a hearing aid. Strange, too, that he could hear some fuzzy static out of them. Oh, well. He might as well find that on switch. Seesh! These lenses sure were dark.

His finger hit the magic spot. A blister of yellows and greens smacked him square in the eyes, one at a time. Blue faded in through the oddest-looking blotches. They soothed Damon's eyes like gentle spheres of ice.

He blinked the glare away. Weird! The reds didn't burn.

Damon scanned in all he could from this congestion, angle by angle, step by step. He could shape out practically the whole forest for about a kilometer. Every single tree had a shape and a colour of its own. There were variants of green. Heck, he could even see the shape of the leaves with these goggles. A batch of birch sprouted here, a mighty oak there. He sucked in all the air he could.

Wickedly cool!

A great shiver rolled over the room. It rattled the deepest bones in Damon's body. A massive blob of yellow drifted overhead. Its movement matched that of the rumble. *That's one mother of a ship to be floating around here*, Damon thought. Maybe the Amazonian—Dad—missed something. Maybe he came back to pick up all these things.

But the ship moved on, further down the forest...looks like northeast.

What the...?

Damon couldn't believe his eyes. The goggles registered what looked like the top of a car sticking out of the organic green ground. Dots of red flickered around the car like specks of dust. Damon could never forget the shape.

Zoe's blue sedan.

Blip!

The goggles flashed a red LED at the far corner of Damon's eyes. He followed until the blink turned to a short blob of yellow cascading through the trees. He checked the sky at once. The big yellow had blipped out of view. For how long, Damon would rather not guess.

Blip!

Another yellow cascaded through the trees. Then another. Damon blinked. More yellows than he could count now shifted their way to the bike shop.

What the...? A smack of black struck him dead in the eyes. He pretty near tore the goggles right of his head had it not been for the cascading yellow. Now what in the world would be hiding under the bike shop? Black? What the heck, dude?

The yellows swarmed the bike shop. Loads of bleeps and static hissed in Damon's ear. The yellows seemed to swish to the rhythm of the bleeps. The static started forming the oddest grunts and snorts Damon had ever heard. What did it all mean? Who are these yellows? What if they were not human? He had only one way to find out.

Damon waved his hand before the goggles. A ferocious blob of fleshy pink screamed in his eyes. He jerked his hand away. Big trouble tied his gut into granny knots. Those yellows weren't human, and the last he remembered, he remembered only one Amazonian in the forest. Damon would have spotted him already, somehow. Mom would register that fleshy pink his hands did.

Thunk!

The ground rattled ever so slightly. Footsteps rang in Damon's ears. The yellows swarmed right underneath him. They carried grey blobs in their arms, likely pulse rifles like the grey blob an arm's reach away.

The yellow began to scatter left and right. Damon could feel maybe twenty some feet, but he could only find five yellows rummaging around the main floor. There must be some invisible things walking around, too. Damon nodded to himself. Yeah, that'd make sense. Since when would these goggles pick up everything if it couldn't do anything past straight-faced pastel colours?

He scratched his ears. The static turned to constant whispers, whispers that would drive even the sanest kid nuts. Damon tapped at the hooks, but the static wouldn't leave. Really! How did he hear these haunting sounds?

Blip!

The noise landed right on top of Damon. He jerked his head high only to slap the colour straight out of his eyes. The soft touch of solids against floppy silicon flickered in his ears. It served him right for losing track of his hands.

He scrambled for the goggles. He figured his eyes would take so long adjusting to the dimmest of blue lights. There wasn't a doubt he caught the yellows' attention, too.

Ah, there they were! Damon scrambled them on his head. His elbow hit pretty near every box and gadget along the way. *Careful, Damon!* You would punch a hole in the silicon! He shut his eyes and counted to four. The intensity of the red from these goggles could fry an egg! He waited for the soothing blue to settle before he opened his eyes. Hardly a shade of green struck his eyes.

In its place, the blue etched a strangely detailed model of the bedroom above. Staring at the LED lights in the wall coughed up a blank space. The pastel colours were all gone, too. Ghosts in the shape of human-insect hybrids took their place. They carried four legs each. No wonder Damon couldn't count those footsteps right.

One of these hybrids stood on the floor directly above him. It held its rifle at an odd angle, low and steady.

Ka-thunk!

A splash of water struck the back of Damon's shirt. He curled himself around to find a spray of water leaking through the silicon. A brisk of fresh light seeped through this hole.

Ka-thunk!

Another hole popped through the silicon. Damon's left foot gave off a wild stinging sensation like something had ripped through his heel. He buckled as tight as he could, caressing the wound. Yeah, whatever the hybrid shot, it cut through his clog like a katana.

His goggles bleeped. A teardrop flickered where his foot had been. Weird glyphs popped up in a box. Damon could swear he had seen them before.

Ka-thunk! Ka-thunk! Ka-thunk!

Damon found no time to think. The hybrid still shot at him, step by agonizing step. Its menacing sweep forced him to the wrong corner. Each pass he made was met by a splash of water. Every heartbeat he made pulse his eyes with dread. This hybrid wasn't shooting for kicks.

The static in Damon's ears hissed more than ever. A rolling drone overpowered the pulse of his heart.

"Keep moving," it said. "Sooner or later, your creator...."

"YEAAAAH!"

Damon's head filled with a most horrible scream. He tore the goggles off at once. Forget the dumb visuals! He wasn't listening to that crap anymore. The break he saw, he was going to gun it to the door even if it killed him.

Damon could still hear the static from the goggles. He figured the sound came from some sort of pulse vibration in the hooks. He had heard of the technology before, but not in such small means. His heart stopped beating for a moment. Could Earth have been feeding off alien technology all this time?

The rain of silver tears halted. In its place, a beam-rattling roar split the air. Damon forced his hands away from his ears. Deafness wasn't going to stop him from reaching the door. Nothing would!

He hardly made two steps when light suddenly bellowed over him. Water sprayed over like a cascading waterfall. The force sent his left hand straight into one of the silver tears. He winced in pain, but could not shout. Everywhere he looked and felt, greasy water would surge through his thoughts.

A familiar rasp of dread barked down on him. "Up!" it called.

Damon lifted his free arm from his eyes. The Amazonian perched overhead, tossing two massive boards aside. A sizeable hole in the ceiling showered him with radiance like no other. The beast's scaly flesh shone brilliant as a snake's newborn skin—too bad about those bloody knuckles.

"Who are you?" Damon shrieked. "I want my mom back, you son of a..."

The beast roared a mighty stench over Damon. He reached down with his meaty hand, obviously swollen from some sort of rage. Damon shielded his eyes, only to find himself flailing through the sky. A branch swatted him atop the apex of his head. He didn't think twice to grab it before gravity took over. His last word rang out his breath.

"Cow!"

He clung hard to the tree as much as he could. Damon found it strange how this particular oak had been standing tall the past few years. Its place would have held perfect for the Amazonian to watch anyone from a good long distance. Maybe the beast waited for him to leave.

KRAKK!

The southeast corner of the bike shop blew off in a blazing mushroom. Leaves singed at the very touch of the blast. Damon felt the intensity wave through him like a tsunami. His hands began to swell like balloons.

Damon fretted. His grip slipped about, forcing him to scramble for more branches to dangle from. A few pushes down, he found himself on a wobbly branch. He snagged onto some smaller branches to stiffen the wobble. The less he moved, the better everyone would miss his presence so high from the action.

Shouting weaved through the air—lots of it. Yet not a word could fit with Damon's English. Some words didn't even sound like anything a human could try, let alone any type of animal on Earth. Sure, he'd hear it on some dinosaur movie, but....

The tree shivered anxiously. Damon gripped tighter, blood flowing freely from his wounded hand. He scanned the rounds of the driveway, but the leaves in this tree kept blocking most of the movement. He remember sighting a human of Egyptian royalty—heavy on the shoulder padding, mostly yellow and black stripes when applied—run amok. Only, its head smeared its presence with a most venomous growth.

The Egyptian bug sprouted insect wings from the back. So weird! It launched itself like a bullet into something.... The Amazonian! Ha! The Amazonian batted it like a baseball. It vanished in the trees.

More of those Egyptian bugs went for him, left and right. Again, the Amazonian made swift work of them with either his tail or his right arm. His left arm looked clawed up from something.

Any more bugs? Damon looked. Nope. Not that he'd call out a warning shout to the big man in green anyway. He isn't Dad.

The Amazonian ploughed through the body hole in the front of the bike shop. Damon smirked. He couldn't see how the creature could sit on a bike and ride away. Ha! His school buddies would get a kick out of that story. If only he'd survive this mess to get to school.

Damon winced. No. His friends wouldn't believe him anyway. He muttered at his own failures before sucking in his breath.

Damon's ears grew of that squealing silence. He peeked through the leaves as much as he could. Not a single creature stirred in sight.

Aw, crap! That full-bladder sensation struck him hard in the gut. Not now! Not while they still tried to see him. *Ack!* Did he have to go! Like, got to go real bad! His eyes raced for a fix. Where to go? Where to go?

His eyes spotted an opening at the other end of the tree where the forest really started to bundle together. He shot a quick glance across the driveway. No one would see him. Besides, they were in front of the house, not behind. Now, if he could only scale these branches as fast as he could.

A new thunder blasted him off his branch. He remembered striking the lip of the cottage roof before tumbling like a rag doll to the ground. The worst kind of light blinded him for what felt like forever. He held on that bladder thought for as long as he could. Striking the soft earth face down didn't help much. Quickly, he sprang to his feet, unzipped, and went. Who cared if the bugs were watching? He vowed never to wet his pants again!

Blazing Stones

The bladder emptied, Damon let the blindness settle to the far reaches of his watery orbs. The burning wrinkled like rainbows in the sprat of sulfur and dirt. Wow! Did it stink like sulfur or what?

Yeah, right! Damon smirked. Since when did a blinding flash generate the type of fart only Grandpa would dare to unleash? Like, nearly everyone in his family was allergic to perfume, Damon included.

He stepped gingerly around the house on half a leg. Oh, how his feeble leg swelled when it's twisted even the slightest. The bloody hole in his right hand did little to encourage him. Yet, his curiosity had become his greatest strength—his only reason to push on.

What was that sulfur stink about?

Damon made it two steps from the southwestern corner when he looked up. Man, did it stink really bad! Like the stink from the paper factory down the valley his house used to be in when the wind blows.

What the...?

What happened to the bike shop? And what was with the big flipping crater in the middle of the driveway? The size of it made it look like the atom bomb of garage experiments. Dad would probably fit three of the cottages down this nice hole had he had enough strength.

Oh, wait! He had turned into that Amazonian. He'd probably lift half the spotlight mountain if he could.

Then the sky went "Boom!" Damon instantly remembered his TV lesson on the sonic boom and how it meant that something had broken through the sound barrier. He raised his head as a snail to the radiant sky. A skid of dust streaked out into the stars. A fainter trail of dust came back from that puncture mark. Damon eyed this trail closer. It headed straight back to him.

Dad left in his ship, and he had Mom with him. Not once did Dad even asked for Damon to join him. Not once did he tell Damon the slightest of his alien nature. Mom, neither. She would have had known. Damon should've figured it out the moment she chucked him in the closet. She must've known pretty near everything about Dad. She was still his wife. They shared secrets with each other. That was their nature.

So how much did Mom know about those bugs? The way Damon saw Zoe's car through those goggles, Mom must had known someone targeted them from the start. Why else would she send Zack off with Zoe so fast?

Then the thought came to Damon.

Zack! He was in Zoe's car!

He scanned for a decent bike, only to find the crater. But then, he didn't park the crappy loaner in there. It should still be leaning on one of these trees. Damon won't get much out of it with his throbbing leg, but it would have to do. Damon still had a good couple of years before he could jump into Grandpa's truck anyway.

He made do with another salmon wrap before launching his way down the dirt road. Zoe's car should be a kilometer out where the swamp starts. Why else would there be such a big blob of blue behind it?

This part of the path, ever the most memorable, wound its way around one hill and jogged up a second before dipping into a part-swamp, part-farm field valley. The field usually flooded in the spring, but that year had been the wettest one yet. Even Grandpa couldn't drive to the cottage until the water receded from the road.

Damon eyed the sugar shack at the top of the hill jog. It seemed slightly out of place with all the rotted wood and bars of iron sticking out of the framework. An old ceramic tub hid within the refines to boost the hut's rustic nature. But like the last couple of drive by's, Damon found nothing new to report. He pedaled on.

He spotted the trunk of Zoe's car sticking out of the ground like the sore rump side Dad always took it for. The rest of it seemed sunk in what looked like a wide scorch mark in the road. No doubt it was another crater, and Zoe parked her car right into it.

But none of that. Damon still thought of Zack as the priority issue. He could live a week without Zoe flipping flirts at him. Heck, a whole year without her would be a lot better than a day without Zack. Without Zack, Damon had nothing left to care for. He'd had nothing left to live for. He'd rather be dead long before Zack.

He closed in on the car fast and strong. He deployed himself off the bike, and let it drag its own weight behind him. He'd move faster on foot, his swollen leg long since forgotten. Zoe's car didn't stink of sulfur. Unfortunately, neither did the crater. In fact, the crater had no smell at all. The air felt so fresh here.

So what would cause a crater like this? And why wouldn't Zoe catch it in time? She would have spotted this one well ahead of time, and yet she actually drove straight into it. Damon found no skid mark behind the back wheels, and the way the front's all smashed up, she'd likely gone at the best speed her car could go on loose dirt.

Damon took a quick peek inside. Glass littered the seats everywhere. The driver's seat had its share of blood. The airbags didn't deploy, either. The way the steering wheel was bent at the top, Zoe would have had to be knocked out at the very least. Yet, Damon couldn't find anyone in her seat. He shuffled toward the back. There was no little brat hiding under or behind the seats, either. He popped the trunk and found it empty as the Sahara desert.

"Zack!"

He turned to the swamp, shouting his brother's name. A sharp gait overtook his bad leg, the pain tossing him to his knees. Blood rushed to his head mighty and hard. His heart pounded fiercely against his chest over and over. The worrywarts grew all over his brain. Suddenly, he cared about his family again. He cared if Mom was so brutally attacked by...something. He cared if he screwed up and turned Dad into a monstrous lizard man. He cared if Zack was missing from the picture.

Zack was just one person. He needed his whole family back.

Then Damon caught himself. Why did he even bother? Zack was not going to run around in the swamp. He hated this road. He'd more likely to dip his head in a hot tub cranked at full blast. You couldn't hear a kid scream any louder than that.

Hot tub.... The words stuck in Damon's thoughts. Then a new thought swooped right over. Ceramic tub! If there were anything Zack would run and hide in, it would be that stupid shack. He had done it before, lots of time. Damon curled his lips. Yeah, exacting revenge on a little brat could be one of life's guilty pleasures.

His whole body shivered in frustration. *Focus*! Damon shouted in thought. He said the word like a broken record. Focus! On his bike he hopped, pedaling harder than he had done before. If there were any time to reach out to Zack, it would be now. Damon didn't have to lie like Dad did. Zack knew the truth anyway.

"Zack!"

Damon did yet another skid and dropped midway up the hill. The crappy loaner could take the abuse. He called Zack's name over, reaching the apex of the shack hill. "Zack, I'm sorry!" he cried out as he reached the tub. "I was wrong! Mister Fuzzy's real! I saw him." Damon shot a quick peek in the tub.

Nothing. As if Zack would hide in such an obvious place! Damon sprinted to the shack's rusty entrance, his heart pounding as hard as ever.

He held his breath and sped inside the dank shack. Everywhere, rust and wood rot made dreary art of this place. It reeked like the dampest of mold, like when he rode past a rotten log along his bike paths. Shelves looked like they'd been chopped by the crudest of kung fu masters. Mason jars were shattered all along the floor. Damon minded his step.

"Come on, Zack! You can hear me, right? You know Dad had secrets. You know he'd been talking to Mister Fuzzy..." Damon hesitated. Now how did you make it sound like you know everything to an autistic brat? "They've been talking about stuff." Damon groaned. Real mature, stupid! That'd make the brat shut up for good.

But what did it matter? Words had no meaning when one searched high and low through the scrappiest of huts. Damon's insides leaked with dread. A wrong move—a wrong step—could send this shack crumbling down on him like a pile of bricks. He hastened his pace, only to riddle his palms with wood. Ooh, the agony of infected wood. His hands would be swollen the next morning, if he could survive that long.

Damon grew quiet in an instant. He awaited that long ago due call his brother was meant to say.

I forgive you.

None came. Zack wasn't here. Damon stood right away. The Egyptian bugs must've snatched him and Zoe by now. Why else wouldn't Zoe struggle back to the cottage for at least a phone call? She'd do more than her worth to keep Zack safe. She'd tell someone by now where Zack was. That was, after all, her job.

Out the shack Damon went, prying the splinters out his palms one by one. He slumped hard to his knees. The swollen leg pulsed with anger at each passing heartbeat. He couldn't help it. The sight before him crimpled his gut and made his brain fizzle like boiled salt. He stiffened his chest and shook his fists to the sky.

"COWARD!"

Yeah, Dad was a coward all right. He was such a big coward that he was afraid to tell his own son what had been going on all these years. So far, learning the truth was like stabbing oneself in the heart. Damon bled all over. He bled in tears and in anguish. His whole family was gone—all because Dad was too much a coward to tell the truth.

Damon slid back on the crappy loaner and pedaled home. His mouth begged for much needed water. Any time now, his body would be begging for another stop on the toilet. He couldn't help it if Zack had been kidnapped. He couldn't call the authorities or anyone of that sort without getting the wrong attention. They'd think he had cabin fever.

Well, maybe this Mister Fuzzy won't. He happened to be one of those crazy aliens. Yeah, if Zack were right about this guy, then Damon would probably get all the info he needed to get Zack back. Too bad Damon killed him with that magic stone. Too bad Damon screwed up and made a mess out of his family. Dad wouldn't be a grumpy lizard man now. The cottage would be in one piece. There would be no crater in the driveway.

I am not a freak.

Fitz's words echoed deep in Damon's head. They haunted him like a clutter of ghosts clogging the backs of his ear canals. He never said those words aloud, and yet the creature read his thoughts perfectly. The words pulsed louder than his heart.

I am not a freak.

"Freak," Damon echoed aloud. "I know you're not. So what are you, then?"

Fitz's voice whispered distantly in his thoughts.

I'm a telepath, of course.

The cottage came in clear sight. Damon steered south, away from the amber tint of the log exterior. He couldn't let Fitz's words haunt them like this. He was going to use those words to get back at Zack.

Damon pedaled the best he could with this old clunker. It shouldn't be near as tough treading past these rock gardens and gnarly roots now. Damon felt no more pain. From the moment Fitz's voice steered him out of the rut, his leg had stopped pulsing. It was the right move to make.

Trust the very person who killed Grandpa.

But where to start looking? Fitz wasn't around the fountain after the big flash. Neither was Dad's stone.

Bzzt!

His pants gave such a wobble that his tree plowed into a sharp incline. Damon hit the dirt rolling. His bad leg snagged itself in the bike frame. He could hear his knee crackle as he rolled around to catch whatever buzzed in his pocket.

It was Zack's silver ball.

No sooner did Damon rip the ball from his pocket than it ripped out of his hands and sped through the underbrush. He hightailed after it, limping huge gaits every three paces. His wounded hand throbbed hard, yet it hardly bled. The alien DNA seemed to be patching the hole rather well.

The ball zigged and zagged through the maze of trees like it knew it was going. Damon could hardly believe his eyes. *Now what is doing this?* Damon thought to himself. The ball moved around like someone controlled it with a hidden remote.

But who could be controlling it? Dad? Zack? No, and no.

Fitz? Now, that was a possibility.

Suddenly, his feet hit him with the drench of trickling water. The ground shifted like a bed of marbles. Damon toppled backwards, arms flailing. He felt something jab straight in between his shoulders like the blunt end of a large rounded beam. Muscles seized. Bones cracks. The feeble leg pulsed with furor once more.

It came clear that Damon stumbled along the river's rough shoreline. He didn't imagine himself being here so quickly. Even the undying fortress of trees deceived him.

"Get with it, Damon!" he told himself sharply. "This is no time to mess yourself around." He drew sharp breath, each inducing some sort of sting in his right chest. Yeah, right! Like he actually broke his ribs on a stupid fall like that. But, boy!

Why was it so hard to breathe all of a sudden?

He limped on up the river. He still had half a kilometer to go before he'd reach the right trail. Then he'd have to head up the hill and start looking for Fitz there.

Or not.

He hardly made two steps when he stumbled upon the slickest rock in the riverbed. He hopped a few leeching steps, turned back, and found Dad's elder stone. Weird. Zack's ball had latched on this one like it was with the one still in his pocket. Then a few steps further, a mound of fur broke the surface for a tiny moment. Damon waited, hands in batting position. The mound of fur surfaced again. Yet the water seemed so murky here.

Bubbles tickled Damon's feet. He swatted at the water only to latch on a leg. He pulled up, hard. Half of Fitz's worm dog body followed. Gravity took over. Damon toppled straight into the water....

And all over Fitz like a busted vase. Ack! Fitz's fur tickles like the worst kind of tickler. Damon started swatting again. He reeled and he squawked until he reached a decently carved boulder. Then, with a great thump, he sprawled himself upon his chest. It took about fifteen breaths to pace his heart back to normal.

Sploosh!

Damon jerked his head left. A glitter of blue split through his eyes. He snatched the stone before it could drift down the current. It rattled in his arm.

"Trust the spirits!" a voice whispered. Damon had to double back to keep the stone in his hand. "Trust the spirits," the voice said again. It felt like it came from the stone.

"Trust the spirits, and they will guide you."

The stone talked. The stone actually talked to him. No! No, it couldn't be. Damon struggled with his memories. No, stones didn't talk, no matter how fancy they looked. It couldn't talk.

"Trust the spirits."

It did talk! It either talked or Damon had lost his mind. Yeah, that was it! He had the same vibe Grandpa did with the other stone. These stones made him hear voices that weren't supposed to be there.

Damon dunked the stone in a crevice. His breaths slapped rage against his chest. The blue ember pulsed within the crystal clear quartz. It spoke words to the wind, but Damon shut them out. He scooped up a rock and swung for the stone. He was not about to turn into Grandpa just yet.

KRAKK!

A fireball erupted from Damon's hands. He dropped the blazing stone and spun around screaming. Oh, did his flesh burn! He dunked his hands in the water, but it wasn't enough. He felt the burning everywhere. He tried rubbing his hands, but that only stung. He tried fanning his hands in the air. That was even worse than dipping them in hot oil! Hell, did these hands burn!

KRAKK!

The water surface exploded next to Damon. A rush of heat blanketed his legs. Steam hissed where the water had burst open. He barely noted a hint of boiling red somewhere in the fray.

More explosions spurted from the rocks, left, right and center. Damon zigged. Explosions splashed boiling water at his shirt. He spun around, wailing in agony. More water scalded his arms. He spun back toward the stone. A pair of Egyptian bugs burst out of the burning brushes, arm gauntlets blazing with flames. Their mouths opened like fierce spiders with protruding fang tentacles without the lower jaw. Damon didn't stare at any one mouth for any longer than his stomach could handle. He much preferred their beady little eyes.

One spoke in that stupid language again. Damon retorted with all his might. "LEAVE ME ALONE!" he bellowed madly as he clotheslined the first. He aimed a good elbow for the second, but they swerved away. A mess of limbs shot from the water, their razor follicles tearing through his arm. He tumbled back, raging harder than ever.

"THAT HURTS, YOU PUNK!"

The bug left and, standing simply, tossed a cluster of pebbles his way. He batted them away, only to hear that splendid crack of the bug's rifle.

Suddenly, the pebbles rained fire. Damon lifted his shredded arm just in time. He ducked and rolled to douse the pain. He held his breath long enough to catch a hole in the attacker's stance. He brought his legs over his chest with a hefty shove. A spiral kick ploughed straight into the bug's chin. It went crumpling back like a boulder tumbling down a short mountainside.

"Ha!" Damon gestured. "No wonder Dad clocked you guys!" He gave a swift kick at the bug. "Ever heard of karate lesson, you oversized..."

And then he saw the blade sticking out the attacker's chest. His body froze on the spot. Where did that come from all of a sudden?

"You could use a little lesson on melee combat yourself."

Damon's heart jumped off its casing. He spun around and met the stone thief eye to eye. The worm dog's amber glow pierced his heart like a cheese grater. It was telepathy at its best.

"Who asked you?" Damon retorted.

He spun around, fists swinging. Not one swing connected with the wrinkly worm dog. Damon tried a rebound elbow to the head. Fitz caught it like it was nothing.

Fitz cleared his throat. "Do you mind?" he hummed generously. "I have important..."

Damon caught a new opening between the worm dog's front legs. He drove his left leg up at once. Fitz shoved it straight down with his front leg. The force threw Damon off-kilter.

He splashed and sputtered all the curses he could rattle on Fitz. "Son of a flipping cow!" he hollered. "I'm going to kill you!"

"An absolute lie," Fitz nodded back. "I can tell, the way your eyes float in your head. "Now if you wish, I shall..."

Damon swung his arm for the worm dog's head. Fitz caught it like it was nothing—exactly as Damon wanted. "Don't you tell me I'm lying!" he screeched. He readied his free fist, only to lose sight of the ground. A torrential force drove all the air out of his lungs. The air howled in his winds for maybe half a second.

Then he flew and hit a tree.

What just happened?

He dragged himself to the shoreline in a gag of blood and spit. Now his chest *really* hurt! His arm didn't feel so bad, though.

"Listen to me.."

Damon slumped into the gravel of pebbles. He couldn't bother to look up. The splash of the water told him Fitz headed his way.

"Listen to me!" Fitz's voice roared softly. "You have the right to as many questions as you need, but responsibilities are in high expectations this morning." Damon didn't ask what those responsibilities were. The jitter in Fitz's voice said it all.

"All right," Damon groaned. He sat promptly at the river's edge. "But tell me, what is Zack's worth to you?"

Fitz drew a long breath. His eyes spaced wide, chin rising gently to meet the river's subtle breeze. Damon breathed this gentle air, but could find no pride in this. He'd rather run off with Dad than sit right next to the alien who killed Grandpa. He reminded himself that Dad held back all the secrets, not Fitz.

Finally, Fitz lowered his chin to Damon's level. "He means..." Fitz stopped for a moment. His eyes seemed to be searching for words in the breeze. "Our lord, Emperor of the Known Galaxy, means more to me than you'll ever know." He blinked a while, focusing on ghosts that Damon would never see. His smile opened a row of pine comb teeth, stained and bloodied.

"Now I believe you owe me an egg."

Turbulence

Fitz helped wrap Damon's wounded arm with shreds of worn cloth. Fitz wouldn't say where he retrieved the cloth, but he did reveal something weird about their two stones.

"You simply touch here," he said, poking the stone into Damon's throbbing chest, "and the hidden wounds are reversed."

Damon felt his chest pop more than once. He griped and clenched his miserable chest with writhing pain. Then, as quickly as it shocked him, the pain vanished. He stumbled on words he couldn't possibly speak with so much shock. Fitz tapped his leg with the stone. Another painful snap drew the throbbing pulses away.

Fitz hid the stone away in his backpack with the other. "I have my doubts," he sighed, "but I do not believe the aftereffects are long term. Under your circumstances, you should be able..."

Damon shook his head. "Whatever you're thinking, I'm not that monster. I'm as much a human as Zack."

"More so," Fitz nodded. "That is why I may possibly heal your wounds more swiftly than I have with Lord Zachary in the past. I..."

Damon cut him off. "Whatever your past is with Zack, I don't want to hear it. I just want him back on this planet, safe."

Fitz gave him a stern eye. "And you?" he muttered loudly. Damon stirred. Why did Fitz have to sound drunk half the time?

The great owl eye shivered Damon out of thought. "I'm off to find Dad as soon as Zack's safe," he blurted. "What's the big deal between you and Dad anyway?" he blurted sharply. "He acted like you were going to kill me!"

Fitz looked him straight in the eye. *That piercing telepathy stares again*, Damon thought.

"Did you think I would truly kill you in either case?" said Fitz.

Damon forced his scowl into a scrunched up frown. "Why don't you read my thoughts, then?" he growled. "You've done it enough times already, haven't you?"

Fitz drew a sigh, eyes half shut. "I would be violating your rights."

"Hello!" Damon trumpeted. "Those were my dreams you were hacking into, idiot! Hello? What difference does it make?"

Fitz grew to his feet—all four of them. His worm tail swished behind him like a lowly pet. Depression sank into Damon's heart from out of nowhere.

"We are but sitting ducks here," Fitz announced coolly. "A jog through the forest would be sufficient, don't you think?"

"I'd rather jog," Damon growled back.

They tracked hardly half a kilometer when Damon found himself spilling questions out of his mouth. His questions felt more like marbles made of granite roasting in a frying pan.

"I don't get it."

Fitz stopped in his tracks. His front left leg seemed drifting humbly beneath a brown stain on his shoulder cloths.

"What do you not understand?"

"Could you cut the formal talk?" Damon snapped suddenly. "It's bad enough that Zack talks faddy pop culture."

"Habits are hard to kill," Fitz nodded.

"Well that's a start," Damon answered. His breath channeled a strain of agony from his heart. "So Dad's been hiding on Earth all the time."

"Terra Tetris," Fitz answered.

"Terra what?"

"Terra Tetris," Fitz announced. "This planet is named Terra Tetris. It is the one hundred and twentieth *terran* planet discovered by the monks of the Sacred Era."

Fitz's answer left a shattering taste of bitterness in Damon's mouth. "I don't really care. I'll call it Earth, and you're not going to force it out of me, understand?" Fitz nodded silently. "Good," Damon acknowledged. "Now, Dad's been hiding on this planet for who knows how long.... Don't interrupt me!"

Fitz dropped his weight. Damon went on.

"He's been hiding here for so long, and no one's even gone close to blasting a single hole in our car. Then out of nowhere, you pop out of the woodwork (Dad says that all the time) and start going on about these stupid stones.

"Then Dad goes crazy, starts shooting rock salt all over the place. I try to break you guys up and somehow turn Dad into some kind of monster..."

"Draconian," Fitz grunted.

Damon stared. "Did I hear you right?"

Fitz nodded subtly. "The word of your native tongue has every bit the right..."

"Fitz!"

The worm dog cleared his throat. "Yes, the word fits the species. Go on."

Damon beamed hard. "So all this starts happening, and then these bugs...Don't say it! These bugs start teleporting out of nowhere like spawn points in my video games. And they're dressed up like some Egyptian pharaoh's secret service clocking liquid metal bullets at me here and there. And then these fire bolts! They literally set that rock on fire!"

The air grew stiff. Damon could hardly breathe. He held out his hands and rattled the frustration out of them. His brain ran out of words. Fitz gestured a wide-open mouth and an index finger. He seemed to understand.

"Interesting," grunted the worm dog. "I wonder how many aliens seek refuge on this forbidden planet."

"Say what?" Damon snapped.

Fitz's eyes shuttered like chaotic apertures. "Nothing you would understand until later. Please, what is the question you're trying so hard to ask?"

Damon released it all. He released the pain of losing an entire family. He released the anger he had held on Fitz. It exploded in a massive burst of breath.

"What the hell is Dad doing on this planet if it's supposed to be off limits, hunh?" He didn't give Fitz time to answer as more curiosity struck him as he waited. "And how about you? Why are you here? Not that Dad needs any protection or anything..."

"Your father had a mutual agreement," Fitz announced. "I agreed to parenthood in one mean or another. Azeroth decidedly searched for any loose stones such as these, so long that he offers them to me freely." Words burned as coals beneath his breath. He drew a swift sigh. "As you are aware, he did not follow that arrangement."

Damon limped a scowl aimed for Dad. "And what about Grandpa?"

Fitz's eyes hovered away. "The only person who knew nothing of these affairs is you, Lord Damon. Your grandfather knew more than enough about the stones. He simply ignored my warnings after he realized its healing powers." The worm dog's face began to wonder. "Now what did they call that terminal illness again?"

"Cancer!" Damon snapped. "And you killed him, remember?" A buzzing noise fluttered across his left lobe. He swatted at the mosquito and dispensed itself into nothingness.

"I murdered no one," Fitz sighed. "He shot you when you attempted to intervene. When he did not submit to his mistake, I realized how deep his stone's damage has done."

"Ha!" Damon barked. "So you did kill him!"

"Murder means nothing in combat," Fitz bowed. "My kind does not indulge in such foolish rage. However, I did snap your grandfather's neck. I must say..."

"SHUT UP!" Damon wailed. "I don't want you saying *anything* about snapping anyone's neck again, do you understand?"

Fitz bowed with his index finger pressed straight on his...upper chest sort of place. "I shall abide, my lord. Now, shall we continue on?"

Damon threw an arm. "Yeah, go ahead and get me lost. Not like I'm stupid or anything!" He found emptiness in his broken words. How could everyone know all these craps that had been going on? How could they all leave him in the dark like this?

Fitz rolled his stubby arms together. "Likewise," he chimed, "your stupidity has gained you an advantage."

"Like hell!" Damon snapped. "I don't belong here with you!" He kicked at a gnarly root twice. Why did he have put with this? Why did he even bother to ask these questions? Fitz would only shoot back the dumbest of all answers anyway.

Fitz broke Damon's focus with a deep growl. It sounded more like a kitten's purr than a Draconian's roar.

"On the contrary," said the worm dog, "your stupidity has drawn little to no attention in the many years your father has hid here. Lord Zachary..."

"Zack!" Damon pointed. Fitz moved forth, undeterred.

"Lord Zachary..." Again, Fitz wondered off. "I have no reason to explain his matters. For now, you must understand the circumstances Azeroth has set you against."

"HE ABANDONED ME!"

"Quiet!" Fitz hissed. "The Buzzards...Egyptian bugs as you call them.... They are unmatched in their hunting capabilities. Only they would be capable of tracking your father down to this planet."

Damon crimpled his face. "I thought you said this was a forbidden planet. This planet's supposed to be stock full of illegal aliens anyway. No, you don't have to ask why I'd know that. I do have to ask: Wouldn't these Buzzards think to look here first?"

"Uh, no."

Fitz seemed to take a while to give that answer. Damon could hardly wait for his explanation. He continued to swat around his ears. Where were these mosquitoes coming from? It was too late in the game for the ladies to be sucking on his blood.

Fitz rambled on. "This planet is considered to be of sacred value to the Empire. It has been for countless generations. No one is allowed to touch it, regardless of how much good they could get out of their actions."

Damon snorted a booger. "Let me guess. Immigration."

Fitz shook his head sternly. "Asylum, actually. Exile, if you wish to push it. Those who hide here..."

"End up like Dad," said Damon. His heart pulsed with guilt.

"Again, no," Fitz groaned. "Azeroth was a special case. As I said, we shared a previous arrangement, one that started with a rescue operation and one that ends as we speak." A pause. "You are aware the Buzzards have not yet left, no?"

"Unfortunately," Damon sighed. "I didn't think they'd take after Dad without trying to salvage the rest of my family. One of them shot some sort of liquid metal pellets at me, too. Almost felt like they were toying with Azeroth...err, Dad."

"He was," Fitz said in a gentle whisk. "The Buzzards have their ways of weeding out the truth in out of their preferred clients, Azeroth being one of them."

"But why me?" Damon pondered. "Why Dad, even? You did say something about an exile, right?"

Fitz drew a long sigh. "Azeroth assumed exile because I deceived him. I require these stones." He waved his own stone out of the backpack. "They are for a ritual I intend to perform sooner than later. Many lives depend on the outcome."

"And let me guess," Damon rolled on, "You'd rather keep zip on that, too."

"That depends on our outcome," said Fitz. "We now require these stones for a more immediate task, four of them to be precise."

Damon beamed with pride. "Good!" he chimed. "So it's not going to be another Mario Brothers coin hunt." Fitz gave him a blank stare. Damon realized his error. "You're not as culturally prepared as I thought."

"Alas," Fitz hummed, "I have found myself secluded in your grandfather's lot for far too long. I have lost touch with the extremities of Terra Tetris as I have on many accounts with the rest of the Known Galaxy. Recently, however, I have stumbled onto some startling connections with the underworld."

Damon tossed his shoulders high. "Figures."

Fitz began to wobble to the left. He seemed annoyed by something, maybe these stupid bugs hanging around Damon's ears.

"It appears that an unknown had identified you as a hybrid of special circumstances," said the worm dog. "How they have learned of your leg mending itself at an unnatural pace, I would have no idea. What is important is that the Buzzards had been alerted to intervene with your life at the empress' request."

"Royalty sucks." Damon snapped. A nerve stretched in his brain. "Wait! You said Zack was the emperor! What gives?" His voice wondered off as his hands swatted about his head. "What the...?" He scowled. He swatted his earlobes full force. The buzzing remained. "Stupid bugs!" he ached. "Where's the bug repellant when we need one?"

Fitz withdrew what looked like a bladed baton. Damon shot his arms up at once.

"Isn't that a little excessive?"

"Hold still," Fitz commanded, stepping forth with one eye shut. His stubby arm held the baton like featherweight. Damon blinked. Fitz aimed for the head. Damon lurched back, his gut reeling with sickly intuition.

"Oh, no you don't!" Damon exclaimed too late. Fitz punched at the air, grazing Damon's temple like a paper cut. Damon yelped aloud. He clenched his new wound sternly and took a swipe for Fitz's baton. The worm dog hid it as swiftly as he blinked. How the blade fit itself in without puncturing the backpack was beyond Damon's thought.

"Hand from your wound, please," Fitz commanded sharply. "We must test..."

Damon drew a fist for the worm dog, only to swipe the air before the cat-like snout. "Idiot!" Damon snapped aloud. "We use fly swatters on this planet!"

Fitz looked as confused as a pug. "Fly swatters wouldn't leave a minute scratch in their armour," he retorted in his gentleman's tone.

"Not the Buzzards!" Damon crowed. "The mosquitoes! You swing at them like...like this." He picked up a broken twig from his feet and swung at the air. Fitz blinked a mile a minute. He looked no less confused than before.

The worm dog swiped the twig from Damon's grasp. "Fool!" he barked in a whisper. "The more you move, the more excessive your wound becomes!"

Damon snapped a leaf from a cluster of weeds. He wiped the side of his face until the leaf turned a violent red.

"There!" he barked back. "Is that better? Seesh!" he stammered to the side. "What'd you do that for, anyway? *Gah!*"

"Hold this to your wound."

Fitz plucked a frosted orb from his backpack. Within elbow's reach, this orb looked about half the size of the stones. It looked more modern yet hollow.

"What?" Damon blinked. "You're joking, right?" He snatched the orb and held it against his temple. "Well, it's not a rag, but I guess it'll..."

No sooner did the orb touch the wound than the buzzing stop. In its place, a blood-chilling scream rattled through Damon's bones. The scream rattled for some time, changing into frequent words so sharp and cruel.

God help us all! The spiders! They're everywhere! They're dropping us like flies down here! Somebody please help us!

Damon dropped the orb at once. He meant to spit a curse or two, but Fitz's awkward reflex stopped him. How this tipsy worm dog can catch stones two inches from striking a tooth rock drew Damon breathless at all ends.

Fitz held the orb to the sunlight. It looked more solid all of a sudden. "Blasted sunlight," he cursed sharply. "I would have expected the spirit to exhaust more energy." He stuffed the orb back in place. "It will do for a short period..."

"Knock it off!" Damon hollered. "Straight answers, please."

Fitz seemed to snap out of his scowl. "I apologize," he crackled. "I was expecting more light out of the spirit. What was it you asked?"

Damon's brain went limp. "A spirit? You mean a ghost?"

Fitz threw an arm. "Pah!" he exhaled. "I would expect better of your wording. Yes, it is a spirit. No, it is not a ghost as your kind constantly claims. Ghosts are not of existence. Well, not in this universal dimension, as far as I am aware."

Damon stared. Fitz might be sure of himself, but was he always right?

"No, you see..." Fitz gave a subtle cough. "I find myself searching for spirit light every two of your earth moons or so. The lost spirits of this planet are somewhat weaker than they used to. Their lights will last maybe about five to seven years..."

Damon sighed a wind of relief. At least that was not Grandpa in the orb.

"Now," said Fitz, "Shall we seek out my old cavern?"

Damon checked his temple for blood. Nope. The wound must have stitched itself after he'd put the orb on it.

"Wait a sec!" he blurted out. "If that's a spirit you caught..."

"Oh, I do apologize for the inconvenience." Fitz gestured like some girly guy at a stage production. Twirling his stubby hands in the air then gesturing one in front of the other? This had better not be the norm for his species.

"Spirits may only speak through the blood of a living soul." said Fitz as he tipped his head to the side. "Why? Has the spirit warned you of impending dangers?"

"Yes!" Damon exclaimed. "Yes, you stupid brain dead..." He stopped for a breather, quickly shivering away the excess fear. Push by push, he rose from his knees, brushing away any dirt from his pants. "Yeah," he sighed. "Yeah, it sounded a little weird, though. Something about spiders killing humans."

"Ah, the tomb!" Fitz announced aloud. "That would explain the feebleness of our spirit. I wonder if there are more to spare..."

Damon wanted to puke.

"Tomb!" he cried. "What tomb?"

He stopped. "Is that where Grandpa died?"

Fitz nodded his head.

Damon returned the nod. "But it wasn't the spiders who killed him, right?"

Fitz giggled. "Oh, no. The spiders would have not leaked out of the hatch this soon. Most are still in their incubation process."

Damon stared a long time. He searched for an answer somewhere in that abyss he called a brain.

"Never mind that," Fitz breathed. "We must hustle to the mines before the Buzzards are to make sense of their dead."

Damon rolled his tongue in his cheek. Well, fine! That sounded like a swell idea—jumping out of the frying pan and into the fire.

Yet, as Damon double checked his answers, he realized one truth. If he was about to jump into a fire for something as ridiculous as a stone, would he have to leap to the polar opposite just to save Zack?

It sounded almost too risky. Damon knew this because of what he remembered from science class. Any type of superheated glass will break if it's cooled too quickly. Human hears carry that exact weakness.

He crossed his fingers and hoped his heart wasn't human for the next little while.

Spiders!

"And here we are."

Damon suddenly realized how short he was.

They took the better part of a half hour to reach the cavern mouth, still so awkwardly skewered by the cave-in. Fitz started showing off his so-called magnetic glove, pulling the boulders out like rough Styrofoam. Damon pressed against his belt buckle. Sure the rocks leeched with metal, but were they really that strong on the magnetic meter?

"Of course not," Fitz nodded subtly. "Your body happens upon enough magnetic properties that I can propel you back and forth at will."

"Don't even try it!" Damon snapped.

"Not for some time," Fitz answered, pulling out the last of the boulders. He pulled out what looked like a mini-radar on a post and stuck it in a crack. The radar blinked a little. Damon blinked back.

"What's that supposed to mean?"

"No time," Fitz hurried. "Keep close, please."

They scurried into the cave like rats. Maybe these Buzzard mercenaries would be fleas off that giant cat of an invisible ship. Damon shook the thought from his memory. The cavern walls glowed a poisonous amber for some reason.

"This..."

Fitz said nothing as he revealed the orb. It spat poisonous amber. Then Fitz went on about spirits being a stronger yellow. "This one was obviously poisoned," he mumbled loud enough for Damon to hear. "I wonder if those miners Azeroth heard of disturbed one of the nests..."

"Shut it!" Damon barked. "Let's hurry up with the treasure hunt, okay?"

"We mustn't rush this matter, my lord," Fitz warned sternly. "The incubation nests can be somewhat unstable once I break the seal."

"What seal?" Damon smirked.

Fitz stood Damon before a circular hatch no shorter than one of those bigger blow-up swimming pools. Pour in a truck's worth of lumpy cement and paint a few glyphs along the outer rim with glow-in-the-dark red, and voila! You would get a rather lame tomb entrance to boot.

But, yeah, those glyphs again! Why did they keep popping out of the framework of everything that didn't fit with this planet?

Fitz reefed open his mouth, but Damon cut him off.

"The sooner we're out of here, the better."

Fitz carried the orb to a hole in the cavern wall. He deposited the orb into this floor like a quarter. Odd! How come Damon didn't notice it before?

A beam of light billowed from the slot. Suddenly, lines of light formed in the floor, then across the walls and around the hatch. Weird how Damon couldn't notice all the quartz in this cave before, especially the monster orb at the center of the hatch. How'd that get there anyway?

Fitz pointed to the orb in question. "Our key of entry," he sighed. "I believe you own a certain orb of interest. It will help me to open the hatch."

"Orb?" Damon spat. His body slithered into shock. Since when did he have anything useful for this cave?

Wait a sec! Zack's metal ball! Damon dug deep in his pant leg pocket and pulled it out. Fitz snatched it in a heart's beat. He slapped the ball straight into the marble orb. The ball sank in as if the marble orb was made of some sort of stone jelly.

"Now observe," Fitz grinned. He slapped the palm of his blocky glove against the metal ball and twisted to the right. Stones cracked. Dust sprinkled from the ceiling. Damon sneezed. Then he realized Fitz twisted the whole hatch clockwise. The massive chunk of rock acted as thought it had been well greased all these years, but Damon knew better. Funny he didn't notice the glyphs on the hatch lip before.

He watched as Fitz aligned the glyphs one by one. It sort of reminded him of how some of his video games made some of the more elaborate tomb lock act like the twist-and-turn style money safes. He had to stop and wonder for a moment: so who invented that old stroke of genius first? Humans or the other guys?

The floor rattled deep. Damon almost felt like dropping a load in his pants. Wow! If they felt that sort of thing down in California, he was sure Dad picked the Canadian Shield as a hideaway. Damon would have to change his pants every time there a slight tremor rocked his way.

Fitz withdrew the metal ball. He stepped back to Damon's place and offered the ball. "It'll be safer in your hands." Damon took the explanation with relish. He guzzled the ball in his pant pocket. Too bad he couldn't see how the Buzzards could use it against him.

Their eyes returned to the hatch. It split itself into three wedges and withdrew into the walls. Clouds of dust sprouted everywhere, discouraging Damon's sights from the bowls of this new path. He pictured seeing this in a game before. Or maybe he'd seen in his drawings.

Damon rubbed his eyes with vigor. Man, did this dust irritate!

Fitz locked a curious gaze for a moment. "When did you start?"

Damon blinked. "Start what?" He knew Fitz meant the drawings. Still, telepathy?

Fitz bowed in half a gentleman's manner. "Your drawings, of course. When did you start noticing their connection to your adventures?"

Damon thought for a moment.

"Never mind the thoughts," Fitz sighed. "Keep close and don't touch the walls."

Damon blinked. "Spiders?"

"Spider nests," Fitz corrected. He stepped into the cradle of dust. Damon followed with sharp footing. A spectacular hint of blue met him in all directions. *Blue quartz*, he thought. Those gem hounds in Bancroft would've went nuts if they found something *this* rare.

They hardly made it a few feet in when steep stabs of glare struck Damon in the eye. He swatted at the glare, only to feel a brisk swat himself.

"Don't touch the walls!" Fitz repeated sharply. "They're covered in nests." He pointed to the glowing walls. Only, they weren't glowing near as much as Damon had thought.

Nearly half the walls were covered with a sickly white glare. Within these miserable glares rested hundred of clumps, each of them lumpier than a toad's back. A sickly layer of silk—or something—riddled these clumps like a second skin. It made Damon's stomach curdle to the left.

"Keep moving," Fitz suggested. "Your feet should keep your thoughts busy."

Good suggestion, Damon thought. He followed but four feet back from the tip of Fitz's tail. It dragged behind the worm dog's body like a depressed rag doll.

"Does that bother you?" Damon asked. He couldn't help it.

"I was crippled in battle once," Fitz said, undeterred. "My nerves will come back to me from time to time."

"Did it quit on you when you needed it the most?"

"You mean sideswiping?"

Damon nodded intently. Fitz returned the nod.

"You'd probably notice some scars along the side. Yes, I've been liberally saved by my genetic construction."

Damon quacked. "You make it sound like your...body...is a bad thing."

"It wasn't intended to be," Fitz sighed. "I had an enemy or two who knew the weak points carried by my kind. One enemy still does."

Damon buzzed an eye up at the ceiling. "One of the Buzzards?"

"The empress."

Damon nodded, "Oh." Somehow, Fitz's answer didn't digest right. Didn't he mention Zack as an heir?

They treaded on some more. Damon couldn't tell how fast they were going. Something about the nests made it hard to tell how far Damon stood from these walls. Every time he swayed or lurched to the right, the walls would come straight at him as if they wanted him to disturb those eggs. He'd put his arms straight back down and stand straight up. "Not this time," he'd tell himself sharply. He was not going to kill anyone else, even if he couldn't get to that one last stone.

Fitz's tail began to swish. "Just in time, too," mouthed the worm dog. "It appears you're not so focused, my lord. Have the spirits of your troubled past...?"

Damon went red at the face. "Shut it!"

"Very well," Fitz lipped. "I must warn you, however, that you are past due your commitment to the laws of the Known Galaxy."

"My backside, I am!" Damon stormed. "Now where the flip is the stone?

A flash of light bled red across Damon's eyes. A speck of grizzle spattered on his cheek. He wiped it off, quickly noting the suddenly stingy texture creeping across the side of his face. A nerve pulled his finger toward his mouth.

"Don't lick it!" Fitz bellowed. The butt of his baton blade pushed up against Damon's chin. Damon jerked his hand to the side, brushing the excess against his pants.

"Okay," Damon whimpered.

Fitz growled. "Do you know how quickly they've fallen from mere touch?" He pointed somewhere out of this tunnel into a wide span of icy mist. Within the mist, Damon could barely see the outline of miner caps and pickaxes. A blink further and the outlines became skeletons, badly gnawed by what looked like the tiniest fangs in the world.

Damon crimpled his face. "Kindly draw that stick of yours back!"

"Oh, certainly," Fitz hummed aloud. His eyes widened as if to hint a state of authority. "The next time, you'll be missing a few fingers." His baton disappeared entirely, once again demonstrating the unnatural capacity of Fitz's backpack. Now, how much could he stuff in there?

A side thought crossed the back of Damon's thoughts. He meant to speak up, but Fitz caught him with yet another frosted orb. This orb, it seemed, hosted what looked like a metallic torch handle...or claw, or something. He waved it at the mist. The mist vanished in the range of the eerie blue light. Talk about cool.

"Do not lose this." Fitz pointed to the torch claw. "Your brother had the misfortune of misplacing half of my precious metals on more than one occasion."

"Metals?" Damon balked. "You mean...liquid metal?"

"Quiet!" Fitz snapped. "Keep hold of it and be aware of your footing."

Damon snapped his eyes to his feet. Sure enough, he had stepped into a loose clutter of eggs. It was funny he didn't notice them crawling up his body before. He swallowed his pride. Maybe they would've stung him if he did notice. He'd be dancing around like a girl scout tangled in a spider's web.

"Okay..."

Fitz's voice grew suddenly gentle, again smashing his mean streak into a fluff of a thousand flower petals. The worm dog stood firm on his hind legs, holding nothing but a block of metal. *Liquid metal solidified*, Damon thought. He smirked at the idea of parodying a game character. Hmph! Maybe if there were snakes in this cave, these walls wouldn't be so clustered with spider eggs.

"Pay attention!" Fitz barked. "Beyond those bones is the sacred tomb. You should have no problem spotting the stone, but you will need your claw to extract it. Just give a twist like I did with the door..."

"Can't we use your glove?" Damon blurted.

"No," Fitz growled. "You do not yet harness its capability. Nor do you...?"

Bleep! Bleep!

Fitz pulled a new device from his backpack. He took two winks at it and cursed.

"What?" Damon scowled.

"I miscalculated," Fitz sighed. "Straight to the stone with you. Avoid stepping on the soul stone if you can. Too much vibration can send the eggs out of their incubation period..." He blinked at his noisy device. "Never mind that. The more noise we make, the better we can discourage the Buzzards from following our steps."

"What?" Damon ejaculated. "What do I have to take out the spiders?"

"Just go!" Fitz commanded.

Damon sprung to his feet. He ran into the open, stomping as hard as he could in his frantic pace. His mind raced with a thousand needles and no thread to tie them together with. Fitz couldn't keep his personality in one piece. Why couldn't he say the Buzzards were coming after him? Why must he act like a girly man one minute, then a drill sergeant the very next? Was that how a worm really act underground?

Fitz's voice chased him from somewhere in the black behind.

"Keep to your orb. The spiders are discouraged by its deathly glow!"

That's better, Damon thought. He pushed harder on his deliberate strides.

He hardly made two strides past the first of about a dozen lines when a stream of heat reached his shoulders. He gazed upward for a moment, long enough to spot what looked like a rustic star chart engraved in quartz and rock. The stars looked blotchy and few.

The chart itself was circular and divided into three, maybe for wedges. Only the forth wedge looked more like a couple a smaller sections. A lonesome green light flickered in one of these sections. Most of the remaining stars illuminated a brilliant blue-white. Only a few sparse stars glowed a fierce red.

Damon lost track of his right foot. He tumbled face first to the floor, releasing his torch claw in the process. A quick skip and a hop forth sent him back on pace, scooping the torch back in possession along the way. He stomped at the ground, sending shockwaves of pulsing pain through his legs. Any harder and his bad leg would fall apart.

At last, the mist broke completely from sight. An obelisk broke from the darkness, absorbing the haunting glow of the star chart high above. The obelisk stood on three stubby legs, almost like a tree with no solid trunk. Its peak acted as a spike that extended into an acute overhang lowering itself about a third of the way. A massive ball hovered in place, about two hand spans away from the cup at the end. The orb had this distinctive blue glow to it. Damon didn't notice it on his way in, and yet here, before the nearest leg of the obelisk, the orb shone brilliantly.

Several capsule-shaped pods stuck out from the base of this well curved obelisk. Damon counted two from this angle. There might be one more on the other side. Not that he'd know. The treasure stone stared right at his face, a quarter ways up from the nearest pod.

The grand display seemed to hover from the ground the way the last circular line beamed around the base. So flimsy this line felt. It might've been one of those holograms Damon heard about in his games.

Damon counted the twelfth line, one of three steps leading up to the central display of this tomb. Damon wondered, "Who could be special enough to be buried in a place like this? And how would their spirits feel if their bodies were mowed down by these spiders long after death?"

Better not disturb the tombs, Damon shivered. Fitz will go off the deep end.

He dropped his pace enough to scan the obelisk. The stone was stuck in the marble all right, exactly like the squishy stuff back at the main entrance. Too bad he couldn't quite reach it.

Damon readied his torch claw. He wiggled and twisted at the spirit orb, but it wouldn't come loose. He turned to the mist and called out. "Hey, Fitz! How do I...?"

A sting of pain crossed his foot. Damon kicked at a spider gnawing at his ragged shoe. More spiders took its place. Damon stuck the spirit orb down at once. "Back off!" he commanded, and the spiders rolled away. Damon thought he heard a nursery full of babies wailing off in the distance.

Click!

The claw opened wide, dropping the orb against the smoothed blue rock. Okay, Damon blinked. He took a breath, maybe two before setting sight on the obelisk. But rather than a quartz stone encasing a blue ember, Damon found a layer of hoarding spiders creeping downward from its peak. They seemed to be avoiding the red glyphs further up. Weird.

Damon swapped the torch claw in his lazy hand. He better use his lefty for the spirit ball. His fingers clung on the frosted surface like suction cups. He held high and strong, tapping madly at spiders until they broke into the darkness. "Stay back!" he barked, tapping and tapping until....

All of the world left Damon in a body-snatching squeeze of pain. His shoulders slammed hard against some sort of rock first, then his head and arms. His left leg twisted against his well, cramming beneath and behind him like some limp tentacle. He could hear his knee pop. Fitz's voice stumbled through the darkness. From which direction, Damon couldn't tell.

"Do not get any ideas with the spirit orb!" cried the worm dog. "The obelisk will repel any unwanted visitors from the spirit portal."

Oh, great, Damon muttered quietly. He scattered to his feet, left hand slipping on the upward drive. One pace in and he realized the spirit orb stuck to his palm. He went to pry at it, but it only brought him as much pain as the spiders were bloodying his feet all up. He kicked at the few not so fortunate to scurry away.

Off he went, skipping on a throbbing leg whenever he could. Reaching the platform was nothing. Snatching the claw with his lazy arm was something. The spiders kept stinging at him from everywhere. Something about their venom wanted to force music out of his lips. He could sing the entire *Di-Ba-Da-Go* soundtrack!

Damon coaxed himself to sing. Dad wasn't there to stop him.

"That better not be singing I hear!" Fitz warned from the darkness. Damon bit his tongue. He prodded at the spiders with his feet. The spirit orb seemed to be losing its effect for some reason. If he could only reach the stupid stone.

Maybe if he could hoist himself off the lip of this pod, he could plant and twist the claw at the same time.

Click!

The trick worked. Damon jammed the claw in the little grooves housing the stone. In his little swing of face, he twisted the stone out, only to slip from the claw's handle. He should've known how sweaty his palms were.

Oops.

Damon's feet disappeared from under yet again. This time, the pod he struck tumbled with him, rolling a mass of marble and stone right on his arm. The entire leg sounded like rice cereal crackling loudly in milk. Damon reeled hard with pain. He grabbed the stone and the spirit orb from the floor. Stone in pocket, he began tapping at the obelisk. Sure enough, it repulsed his interest.

The shock drew him back on the base floor, minus the tomb lid. His leg crumpled crudely around his back, bloodied and pulsing as hard as ever.

Damon couldn't move. His sight began to ebb away. The star chart hung above him, looming like the largest Christmas decoration he'd ever seen.

One last thought crossed his mind. That little green dot.... It must be home.

A Meal of Rodents

He could hear someone breathing in his ear. He tried swatting at it, but it remained persistent. Besides, the spider venom had locked up his joints like they were metal gears caught in a torrential downpour.

Fitz's voice thundered in his ears. "That's a fine mess you're in." Damon jittered, but his limbs could do no more. He could only moan when he really wanted to shout out at the worm dog. Didn't anyone in the galaxy have manners anymore?

"Your leg..." Fitz broke off. Damon knew what would happen next. He tried biting at his lip and his tongue, but his jaw wouldn't cooperate. The spider venom mixed well with his blood. Well, at least his heartbeat didn't skip.

Oh, hell! The pain! The instant Damon stiffened, he knew Fitz had rearranged that leg. It would have to be straightened if the stone was going to work properly.

"Try to breathe normally," Fitz instructed slowly. "The last thing I need is for you to go into cardiac arrest."

No kidding, Damon thought. His tongue tasted so bitter all of a sudden....

"Okay," said Fitz. "Just a tap here and you'll be able to stand. But from the looks of your face, I'd say you licked your fingers."

Did not! Damon barked in his head. Didn't Fitz trust him?

"The stone can only do so much at this point. The venom's not a solid impairment."

Damon groaned. His eyes throbbed, too swollen to open. He shuffled closer to Fitz's voice. Every word he tried to speak shot pain all over his chest. He was lucky he could breathe at all.

Everything left Damon in a sudden tumble of words and movement. Fitz must have been working out with his arms. Too bad they felt more like teeth rocks on Damon's spine.

Oh, wait! Fitz still wore that plated armour on his limbs, right? Still, he'd need a bit of strength to scurry around like it was nothing. Damon wondered how much it'd take for him to reach that level.

"On the contrary..."

Fitz's voice broke out like a raging fire. Damon shot up from his bed of rocks, only to be struck with the ultimate vertigo. He withheld the impulse to vomit on the spot.

Hmph, he smirked. These rocks feel a little warm, much warmer than a few moments ago. In fact, the whole tomb feeling had up and left his heart in what could very well have been a faint flash of hope.

Wait a second! Where was he? This wasn't the tomb! There was no quartz anywhere in this cave. Well, it felt like a cave, but with plenty of moss along the floor. *Weird*, Damon thought. He'd never seen the moss spread on rock so smoothly before. It was as though someone had pulled an entire blanket of the fuzzy stuff across the entire mass of the cavern's floor. Yet it didn't run up the cracks in the walls like it ought to. Yeah, weird all right.

"On the contrary," Fitz crooned. "You've already developed enough strength to confront a handful of Buzzards on the spot."

Damon focused on his blurry vision. That swishy feeling in his head can wait. Leaning on his better hand for support, he rubbed the blur from his sights, one eye at a time. Sharp details jutted out of the wood works...rather, rock works. A brilliant glow of coal and strained firewood danced around a hunched form of fur and...no, simply fur.

"I should know," Fitz continued, uninterrupted. "You handled yourself much better against those last two than I'd expected."

Fitz had hardly a piece of cloth on his lumpy body. His armour had been cast aside to his right. Damon noticed blotches of fur missing from his back, likely reminders of those galactic battles he'd been hinting all along.

A blunt crunching sound crackled through the dense air. Fitz seemed to be eating, but what, Damon couldn't tell with the worm dog's back facing him so bluntly.

Damon went to speak, but his tongue met empty words. A rash of familiarity blindsided him like a gale of hail. He had been in this cave before, long before he remembered anything important in his life. That first baseball game with Grandpa, was it?

"I see your joints are back online."

Damon coughed.

"Was that meant to be a laugh?"

"Shut up!" Damon hawked. His coughing fit sent jolts of agony through his fingers.

"Water jug's next to your bed," Fitz waved. "Don't mind the taste. I enhanced its flavour with the herbal remedy I mentioned back in the cave."

"Sports bottle," Damon corrected. It looked like one of Dad's from the bike shop. He yanked open the nipple with his teeth and squeezed a nice bit into his mouth. The taste consumed his lower jaw like some numbing gel.

"Tastes bitter, doesn't it?" said Fitz.

Damon wiped his chin. "Actually, it tastes like Grandma's strawberries."

Fitz turned half his head toward Damon. The worm dog's amber eye seemed swollen.

"I would have liked to meet her."

Damon grunted. "She's still alive, if that's what you mean." He poked at the moss with a loose trig. "Doubt she'll let you past the front door without calling the police first."

Fitz nodded. "Understandable."

Damon finally spotted a meal waving in one of Fitz's front feet. It resembled that of an overcooked rodent of some sorts. Fitz pointed it Damon's way.

"By the way," hummed the worm dog. "I expected better intellect amongst the wildlife here. They're not too keen on heeding my warnings."

Damon ripped a subtle scowl. "You're telepathic, right? What's that all about." He began shifting his weight around this lump on his backside. "And where are we, really?"

"Where your family began," Fitz thumbed. "However, that's beside the point. Happy birthday, by the way."

"Thanks," Damon waved. "I think it was yesterday."

"Ah, yes," Fitz nodded. "In any case, I should think to erect a rodent repellant by the tombs next time. Those troublesome squirrels drew more alarm out of me than an entire hive of Buzzards. Even the spiders didn't know what to think of them.

"Mind you, these squirrels did keep them busy on our way out..."

"I'd say," Damon grunted. "Hey, uh...thanks."

Fitz chomped on his rodent. "No need to thank me twice."

"No, uh..." Damon began. Why was it so hard to think all of a sudden? "Thanks for the look out. I'd done the same thing, too, if that was my tomb we'd have to raid."

"Ah," Fitz nodded politely. "I suppose you do understand my reason for not assisting you past the first rite."

Damon nodded. Fitz must have meant the first line.

"Yes," Fitz explained. "My tribe does have etiquette, especially when it comes to respecting our elders. While we're on the subject, you now owe me an egg and an opponent's heart."

"Quit it!" Damon hissed. "I can't give you either of them!"

"Really?" Fitz lipped.

"Yeah," Damon crowed. "And what's this egg business about anyway? I thought that was some stupid metaphor in those dreams you force fed me."

Fitz smiled. "Produce an egg, and I parent the child."

Damon's face went beet red. "How do I...?" His nerves yanked him back, restrained him from finishing such an obvious question. Produce an egg? That was an absurd request aimed at a fourteen year old. Obviously Fitz doesn't know the half about starting families in this civilization. He didn't even know humans don't even lay eggs!

Fitz seemed to have heard these thoughts. He slumped in his seating pose before the crackling fire. Fitz discarded the spoils carelessly amongst the rolling moss. Damon followed its path with his eyes. His stomach begged for food.

He drew in a breath of relaxed night air. How long had it been since he camped out in these woods?

Oh, forget that! His stomach punched him in the brain! "Have any more rodents?" he blurted coolly.

"Here."

A sizable rodent arched over Fitz's shoulders. Damon caught it in both hands. It felt like crisped...burnt pork offerings. Damon felt stupid all of a sudden. Maybe he should opt for some salmon wraps back at the cottage.

"Tastes like chicken," Fitz noted.

"Don't they all?" Damon grunted back. He took a bite off the meal's backside. Hmmm, tasted more like dried pork wedges than the chicken he knew. Dad could do a better job at that than any.

Fitz blew a feeble sigh. "Your father had some interesting means of cooking his meals, yes. I have tasted some of his chicken myself."

Damon shot up to his feet, face boiling red. "Cut that out!" he barked, half choking on his meal. "This telepathy thing of yours is freaking me out!"

Fitz rolled one of his amber eyes over his shoulder. "What do you expect of me?"

"Ask questions, for starters."

"Spoken like your mother."

Damon felt a vein burst in his brain. He mended it before he could spit out the angst it spilled. Talk about maddening. When was this Fitz guy going to let up?

"Second," Damon fingered, "Try assuming a little. Don't get me wrong. You'll get some wrong answers sometimes, but you don't necessarily need to be a mind reader to..."

"Figure it out," Fitz finished. "Yes, yes. I've heard it before. Your father was quite stern on that matter. But forgive me for turning the loop backwards, but I have no intention of making an ass out of you and me."

"Uh..." Damon needn't ask. Grandpa said that all the time.

"Fitz, Fitz..." Damon took another chunk from his rodent. "Just lighten up, okay? You're the only person in my life right now who really knows what's going on...Don't start! I mean, you're the only one who's keeping me from going mental."

Fitz let out a girly chuckle. Damon ignored him.

"I need you, Fitz, more than anything else in this world."

"I thought you wished to plant a baseball in my brain, my lord."

"That's before you proved me your reasons," Damon answered. "Right now, Fitz, I can't walk out of this. I can't show up at an orphanage and say that I've lost my family to some alien disease or something."

"You wouldn't have a choice but to follow me anyway," Fitz fingered. "Do go on. I'd like to see where you're going with this."

Damon felt his body begin to jitter. Damon found no point in holding it back any more. "I want to break out," he said, firm and square. "Snatching Zack from these bugs..."

"Buzzards."

"Buzzards," Damon sneezed. "Fitz, I might sound stupid to someone else on this planet, but I can't let myself to be discarded like bird crap. Even Zack.... He's too special to be left behind for nothing.

"I need to know my family inside out. That way, I'll know where to go next. I'll know where Zack is best to grow up. I'll know where I can settle down after an adventure while he learns to be with the type of friend I'm okay with. Don't start, Fitz. I already know Earth..."

"Terra Tetris."

"Earth!" Damon stammered. "I already know Earth's not safe for us. If the Buzzards know we're here, there's no telling who else would want a piece of this Azeroth guy..."

Fitz nodded faintly. His head turned toward the lick of flames, only to snap back at Damon with curled lips. "Why bother telling me this?" he said.

Damon grew ice fragments on his shoulders. Why did he tell Fitz all of this? It had only been about a day since they started talking to each other proper, and not on the best terms, either. Talk about that fish out of water feeling.

Finally, he spawned an answer on his lips. "Just because..."

"You have a better reason than *Just because*," Fitz sighed. "However, your idea for having me assume things prevents me from going any further with this conversation."

Damon blinked. He couldn't find the words to snap back.

"Eat up," Fitz suggested. "We leave for your grandfather's stone an hour before dawn. The Buzzards shouldn't give us much trouble then."

"Sure," Damon blinked. His head ached for reason. Why did this place feel so familiar?

"You should ask," Fitz grunted. "And then I shall tell."

Damon gave up. "All right," he shook his head. "Have I been here before?"

"Before Lord Zachary was born, yes."

"Ah," Damon winced. "That explains the headache." He scanned the walls and the floor, but didn't find much to help. "This does looks rather roomy..."

"Indeed," Fitz said, patting the mossy lump next to him. "How about pulling a seat here? There are many stories to tell of my abode."

Damon cringed. "No thanks," he muttered faintly. "I'm more comfortable here."

A whimper escaped Fitz's lips. "Suit yourself, my lord." Damon changed the subject.

"I take it Zack was here, too?"

"Ah," Fitz hummed. "Our emperor..."

"Zack," said Damon. "Call him Zack."

"This is where I defy your correction," Fitz grunted.

Damon threw an arm. "Fine. Call him what you want." Fitz let out a faint laugh, a masculine laugh this time. "Our emperor had many meetings here. It was here that I trained many things into him..."

"More like beat into him," Damon lipped. Fitz quivered, hand at the ready. "Ignore me for once," Damon answered.

A fateful sigh. Fitz drew Zack's story in words.

"Lord Zachary..."

Another quiver. Damon bit his lip. Maybe he should turn down the volume in his brain or something.

Fitz went on. "Lord Zachary was taught some of the finest arts crafted in a physical context." He rolled an eye over his shoulder. "You may have noticed his sharpshooting skills to be rather extraordinary.... Or in your case, annoying. At his level, Lord Zachary can dodge most obstacles in a blink.

"Yes, I did beat this into him. It was the one true way to ensure his efficiency under dire circumstances. He hated your father for it, especially with his absence from this cavern. I assure you, Lord Damon, Azeroth had little heart for either of you as humans. He cared more for the Draconian blood that lurks in your body, waiting to explode in a fury of brute strength and durability."

"That's where you're wrong," Damon interrupted. "Dad did have a heart. He showed it to me." He paused—the pain to speak these words. "He showed it to me last night."

"Three nights ago," Fitz announced subtly. "Your recovery from the venom had taken some time longer than I expected."

Damon drew himself from his so-called bed. "Then what are we waiting for?" he fretted. "Let's get that last stone while we're still up and ready."

"Patience," Fitz fingered, but Damon wouldn't have it.

"I lost my patience when my real Dad died," Damon snapped back. "Up off your feet, you lazy pig! We're fetching Grandpa's stone now!"

A Simple Test

Fitz snuffed out the fire. Damon collected the remnants of their meals in a plastic bag he stashed in his rucksack. A few tucks and nips throughout, and they made the cavern feel as new as a mint-condition comic wrapped in illuminate plastic. Fitz even rolled up the moss in a convenient little ball and stuffed it in his own backpack.

Damon cringed at the sight. "Now how do you do that?"

Fitz opened his stubby right palm. It looked like someone etched a triad of circles at the center of his palm. "Electromagnetism is not my only master," hummed the worm dog. Damon didn't bother to ask the rest of his curiosity away. There would be time for real answers somewhere down the road, maybe when no one was trying to hunt them down like a pack of rabid hounds. Damon crossed his heart. That better be soon.

Fitz took the lead from the mouth of the cavern. He straddled his spirit orb around his upper shoulders like one of those chest lamps Zack used to wear. This orb shone much better than the one Damon had to cope with back at the tomb. Too bad the annoying glitter kept getting in the way. It made candles look so clean and...fake.

Damon followed the worm dog's pacing, much to the charge of his pounding heart. They surged their way through the forest, Fitz in the lead. The pressure of rock and dirt against Damon's feet triggered a recent memory. He pounded his pacing harder, simply to keep within earshot of the worm dog.

"By the way," he gasped, "You owe me a bike."

"That is most inappropriate!" Fitz scowled. "Keep your focus on your feet or I'll have to use that stone again."

"That's the thing!" Damon chuckled. "I'd rather ride my bike through this." Fitz gave him the evil eye. "No, really!" Damon pushed. "I'd rather ride my bike through these trees at night. It's much better on the stomach muscles than all this bobbing up and down on my feet."

Fitz growled, "Pah!"

"You'll see!" Damon shot. Fitz said nothing.

They treaded further down the valley shy of the riverbed. It turned out Fitz's cave rested a few hundred steps from where they downed those Buzzards. Damon withdrew every chance he made to ask Fitz how they'd pull off their big task. They still had to take the other stone Damon left hiding under the boiler back home.

Hmph! It wouldn't be a surprise if Fitz had a ship hidden somewhere on Grandpa's lot, too, and it better not be under the cabin, either.

"Watch out!"

Fitz's warning buzzed too late. Damon slammed head first into whatever blocked his immediate path. Damon couldn't see it as the old oak that had doomed the house structure.

Damon reached out with his hand. "Aye Cesar!" he groaned miserably. Some footing ought to shake the fuzz out of his brain.

Fitz's voice came out of nowhere. "Be careful of the exhaust!" Damon shot his arm back at once. He needed only a single hop forward, and all this jitter in his body faded to the back. Did Fitz say something about an exhaust pipe?

"Propulsion exhaust," Fitz answered sharply. "The chemicals on this vessel can be quite toxic to humans."

"Does it give them cancer?" Damon clipped.

Fitz looked stunned. "Yes, actually. One of the rarest types, to be more precise."

Damon nodded a grim sigh. "I thought so."

Fitz's answer alone answered so many questions Damon could never have dreamed of finding the answers here. He wouldn't even have bothered. No wonder Grandpa was all bent out of shape these last couple of years. No wonder he was so paranoid, stock holding old semi-automatics from the base under the cabin the way he did.

After all, who wouldn't be paranoid after some invisible thing in his forest was making him sick beyond belief?

A river of heat flashed over Damon's lips. It figured to get a bloody nose from this leap of faith. He wondered if he'd make it past the better part with all his fingers intact. Or would they grow back the way his skin patched itself after every little cut?

"Over here," Fitz announced from around the bend. Damon could see him quite clearly across this odd patch of dried leaves. However, the worm dog's voice seemed stretched, like it had to carry over a mountain to reach Damon. Hmph! So this cloaking technology did have its flaw after all.

A quiver of dirt tickled Damon's shoes. He hopped a bit to the left, away from this so-called exhaust. He looked up, full of empty words to say. Fitz didn't seem to notice him. A stiff form of lamp light struck his body. What was with the vertical hatch floating above his head like that?

"Over here!" Fitz repeated. "Try not to notice the door until you can see inside.

"Uh..." Damon blinked hard. "Okay, I guess." He made his arch to the light, minding the empty space to his right. Constant reminders of Grandpa's madness flashed through his eyes over and over. Damon vowed not to let his mind break. He reminded himself over and over. He vowed never to let his mind break like Grandpa before him.

Fitz blew a dog-summoning whistle. "You told me to hurry. How about you do the same, my lord?"

Damon picked up the pace. He finally reached the corner of light. It instantly struck him with an invisible glare, sort of like what the sun did to him one nice summer day. Solar eclipses weren't the only things messing with people's sights, so it seemed.

From the hardest angle, it looked nothing more than an invisible light. Drawing closer to Fitz, Damon started to see beyond this light. It reminded him of the portals in one of his games. The corona spewed nothing but light until someone saw straight through the core. Then a whole new world would light up, full with sharp detail and crisp technology.

He noticed a lobby past this eerie light. Well, it looked like a lobby in some high tech mini-skyscraper anyway. A squishy-looking couch on the right broke through most of the metallic glare with a flat out mahogany fabric. *Some kind of leather or silicon*, Damon thought, *maybe like that stuff back in Dad's secret room.* To the left, there looked to be a few storage bins and a locker of sorts. Straight ahead, a circular hatch stood closed and firm. Its fiery amber glare sucked the colour out of Damon's face. Whatever hid behind that hatch, it better not eat him.

"It's the cockpit," Fitz giggled. Damon shot him Mom's stare. The worm dog shut up at once.

Damon pushed his way in. He had to lift his leg high up past the invisible lip brimming with arctic light. Yeah, arctic all right. The light could burn your eyes out, and yet touching it would get you instant frostbite. Talk about wacky science.

Damon made two steps in when Fitz pointed him to the couch. Damon shrugged his shoulders. "Sure thing..."

"Gently!" Fitz snapped as he shut the rear hatch. His warning barely touched Damon's ears too late yet again.

The moment Damon's rump touched the surface, all of gravity sucked him straight in. He grabbed for the nearest ledge before the squishy cushion could swallow him whole. Fitz's eyes jabbed at his very soul.

"I said 'Gentle!'" repeated the worm dog. "That is perhaps the most delicate of silicon mattresses in the quadrant. It responds to even the minutest gravitational shifts."

Fitz's whacked out explanation didn't catch Damon's ears right. "Say what?"

"Treat it like your grandfather's..." Fitz paused in mid sentence. His eyes broke sharp to his right, toward the fiery hatch. "On second thought, I still require your presence in the cockpit." He shuffled his way to the hatch, arms half bent like an outgoing mother of two. "I still haven't the faintest of the last stone's whereabouts."

Damon pulled at the edge of couch. The fabric wants to eat him up. He called for help, but Fitz already slipped through the amber hatch like butter. Damon shook his head.

What a jerk! Damon thought in a course cough. One minute Fitz acted like a rough-toothed fatherly image. The next, he acted more like a woman of staggering concerns mounted to his back. When would that fuzzy worm learn to keep his personality in check? Surely, worms weren't like that at all.

Finally, Damon found the lever he searched for. A handle bar formed past the confines of the crimson cushion. Damon latched on with both hands and tugged. He slipped out of the people-munching cushion like a grainy ball of salt through a pipe of metallic chrome. Ugh! It felt like documents being fed to a paper shredder. Damon vowed himself to use PDAs from then on.

He stepped up to the amber door. It growled back at him.

"Hold on," a voice muttered through the cracks. "I'm dealing with some technical difficulties at the moment."

Yeah, right, Damon thought. *More like personality difficulties.*

His eyes began to wonder across this so-called lobby. The more he noticed the seams and the shell armoured-looking walls, the less this lobby felt fit for a skyscraper. The way the lights creaked through the numerous seams in the walls, and the way a pipe would stick out of the wall here and there. Seesh! This place seemed more like the butt end of a rusty old spaceship of sorts. Damon couldn't find any class, even for the people-eating couch.

"By the way..."

"Ack!"

Damon lunged about, arms swinging. His good fist missed Fitz's nose. Fitz caught the weaker one like a fly on the wall.

"By the way," Fitz moved on, "you should stop pestering your thoughts with this so-called personality disorder. I am what I am."

Damon stared. Fitz blinked with a shiver.

"Right," hummed the worm dog. "I've forgotten your species consists of two genders."

Damon felt sick to his stomach. "And what is that supposed to mean?" He waited for only a second when all heck snapped loose in his brain.

"Forget it, Fitz. Hey, you tell me what I need to do so I can sit back on that couch of yours."

Fitz returned the stare. "You do not feel the type to request such a thing."

"I said no telepathy!" Damon snapped. "I told you it gives me a headache!"

"I was assuming!" Fitz roared back.

Damon pouted his lip. "Fine!"

"Fine!"

Damon scowled for some time. Fitz's eyes did not break from him. Those fierce amber eyes.... Fierce? Ha! Damon could take out that stare no problem. Zack had done worse.

Jerk! Idiot! Who knew an alien could be so clueless? No wonder Fitz wanted Damon to drop an egg on the spot. For crying out loud, Fitz! Damon was not a female. He never had been, never will be. What was this about an enemy's heart? Since when did Damon have any enemies in the first place?

Like never.

Fitz twitched and blinked on every other thought Damon could muster. Clearly, this fuzzy worm had a hard time with his stupid habit—telepathy of all things! Why did Damon have to put up with this?

Suddenly, Fitz pulled a thumb over his right shoulder. "Care to take a seat?"

"Yeah..." Damon blinked. "Sure." He peeked into the cockpit. It stared back at him with a near-empty glare. Other than a central pad of buttons and the works, the room displayed hardly any more than a decent-sized dome for a window. It covered pretty much the entire front of the ship. The ebony tint, however, made it too difficult for Damon to see outside.

Ah, but he rolled his eyes. It'd be another hour or two before the dawn breaks over the horizon.

Damon ignored the dome. Two seats presented their worth, one on either side of the central controls. Each seat looked like it pivoted from a gear set in the ceiling. Kind of cool, but not quite original.

He turned his head back to Fitz's owl eyes. "Which one?"

Fitz stepped off to Damon's left. "The one on the right, obviously."

"Sorry," Damon chimed. "I don't know a thing about spaceships. The right?"

"Yes," Fitz growled. "Take a seat and strap yourself in. A helmet will be provided once the computer's finished taking your measurements."

Damon shivered. He couldn't help but wonder exactly how a computer would take measurements in such an empty room.

Taking a seat was no biggie. The seat rocked a little bit, but Damon was fine with that. He spun around, a little to the left, a little to the right. Who knew his shoes could grip on this lumpy floor so well?

Fitz's voice charged at him from behind a wall of crooked teeth. "Stay still, please." The worm dog sat in his seat like any human would. The chain mail hung far and wide from his many ringed belt strap.

Damon shot a glance. "Come on! I've never been in a ship before. Give a guy a..."

A sudden snag threw him straight laced in the chair. Ebony straps snapped out of nowhere, cradling his shoulders hard against the backrest. Pins and needles draped his arms.

"Ow, Fitz!" Damon griped. "How about some slack?"

Fitz raised his lower shoulders. "You did not yield to my warning. It's your issue."

Damon planted his face in his palms. Oh, great! Not this again.

"In any case..." Fitz drew a long sigh, his right hand hovering over the central controls. "It appears you'll have to allow the computer to scan your measurements once more."

"Well..." Damon sighed. "Warn me the next time, okay?" He sunk his head back. A generous tickle consumed his arms. He withdrew the need to scratch. Fitz looked serious when he meant Damon to stay still. Now how long would this take?

Fitz opened his mouth as if to answer. He shut his trap long before Damon could shoot Mom's stare his way.

The tickling washed away in a blanket of chill. Damon felt every last strand of hair in his arms pluck at the air. This wasn't measuring. Talk about torture!

"Done!" Fitz announced. The worm dog leaned back in his seat, one eye half shut. The other looked occupied over some sort of invisible light. Damon barely caught a cluster of glyphs bouncing off the feverish amber glow.

The shoulder straps gave some slack. Damon stretched his arms out and arched his back until it cracked. Fitz shivered cold in his tight seat.

"That was uncalled for."

"Same goes to your restraint!" Damon snapped back. "Now how about that helmet you were promising?"

Fitz rolled his eyes. "Here," he answered in a high tone.

Damon readied his catch. A decent grab later, he tumbled an oval disc in his hand. It looked like an earpiece with a couple ripped on it. Someone had etched a tiny glyph near one of the narrower curves.

"You put that on your right ear," Fitz pointed. "That was what the letter represents."

"Right ear?" Damon groaned. "Can't I try my left? I'm better that way."

"Right ear!" Fitz said firmly. "We can adjust the settings later."

Damon rolled his eyes. *Whatever!*

He slipped the piece on his right lobe. It hooked on perfectly, almost like those sunglasses did back at the cottage. Damon turned Fitz's way. He could see the worm dog fight with his mouth. Yeah, telepathy could be a pain to break. He must've used it all his life. Sympathy sung in Damon's heart. He didn't doubt Cassie from school felt the same when he couldn't use his hearing aids one day.

A pinch and a trickle of something ran across Damon's head. His nerves broke at the seams, swatting at this pinch like it were a mosquito. Breath after breath, Damon reminded himself: It was supposed to do that.

Fitz looked more annoyed than ever. "I'm waiting."

"What?" Damon snapped back. "Aren't you going to start your ship up?"

"You have the piloting controls," Fitz announced sternly.

"Oh, now you tell me!" Damon scowled. "How about a tutorial then? I'm what they call a newbie back home."

"Just tap the ear piece!" Fitz howled. "Honestly, my lord. I cannot believe you remember so little about your past training."

"What training?" Damon quirked. "All I remember from you are dreams about fried eggs and worms." He added, "And baseball bats shooting out of Mom's favourite kitchen sink. You know, the one I..."

"Tap the ear piece!"

Damon complied, stern and quiet. He let the eyepiece fill him with the bleeding reds and greens. His right ear crackled with that all familiar static.

"Try to ignore it," Fitz suggested, his voice back at a frigid tone. "I left the communications frequency at that level to pick up any sign of trouble."

Damon nodded. "I take it you missed the boat when the Buzzards came flying around."

"No," Fitz said, his voice heating up. "The Buzzards are fools at combat outside their hives. However, their stealth techniques are far superior to your father's."

"Ex-Dad," Damon grunted. "My real Dad's dead. You shot him, remember?"

Fitz threw an arm. "Superficial wounds, my lord. The human hosting your father could never have survived a soul purge, even if the soul had made him immortal."

"You still shot him."

"Are you going to pilot...?"

"Co-pilot!" Damon fingered. "I'm not in the state to drive a ship into the CN Tower, you know. Half the world's still stiff about those twin towers in New York City."

Fitz stared. Damon did not answer. He blinked off the excess red and green. In its place, the forest had lit up before him. Damon winced hard. His gut felt like it'd gone through a dough kneading session. When was all this weirdness going to end? Better yet, when would everything start to feel normal again?

"The talk piece on your ear," Fitz pointed. "Pull it out like a straw. That way, the computer will able to interpret your voice more clearly."

Damon assumed Fitz meant the microphone. He rubbed lightly across his earpiece. He half expected to find a nipple near the lip, but really! Pull it out like a straw?

The straw of sorts slid out perfectly. It even bent itself at Damon's will, ever forming to match the curve of his cheek. Yeah, this technology felt weird. Yet, it could be so wonderful in a new way. Well, at least he didn't have to be so grossed out by this.

He spoke coolly into the microphone. "217 Terrance Crescent."

Nothing happened. Fitz stared straight at him, those amber eyes so icy and distant.

"What form of coordinates are those meant to be?"

"Street address," Damon shivered. "What else are they supposed to be?"

Fitz planted his face in his stubby hands. "I suppose your father has taught you nothing in the slightest." Damon went to cut him off, but Fitz already lifted a finger.

"You see," he said, "we do not share the laziness your human blood inherited. We do not resort to meaningless names or numbers. It shall leave you nowhere but..."

A quiet shiver raked up Damon's back. The forest dimmed before him, his eyepiece alive with meaningless glyphs. He turned his head slight toward Fitz. The worm dog looked stunned or rather frustrated.

"Fine, fine!" Fitz howled over the increasing rattle. "So I've overlooked the recent firmware upgrade." He went on to mumble on about how the controls could read street addresses as he brushed the air with his hands. The glyphs refracting from his owl orbs blinked and changed in all sorts of ways. Damon nodded, "Understood." Fitz's goggles respond to hand movement.

An idea poked Damon like a needlepoint. "Did Dad ever know about this ship?"

"Yes," Fitz coughed. "In fact, he has visited this ship more often than I have of late. The computer should have not responded to your command."

Damon shrugged. "Does this ship have wireless?" Fitz stared. Damon assumed "Yes." He took a breather as his hands clenched into his armrests. "Then I think this computer's hooked to the internet."

"You speak ill of thought," Fitz growled.

"Uh..."

"Do not mind the matter," Fitz shot back. "Keep your hands and arms clear of your goggles' line of sight. I shall upload the ship's piloting tutorials to your goggles. Follow them precisely, and we shall test your capabilities when the convenience arrives."

"Uh..."

Damon stopped there. He'd take Fitz's word for it. If the worm dog can shoot out Shakespearean technical terms like that, then he was bound to know a bit more about theory than Einstein ever did.

A strike of light buzzed through Damon's brain like a seizure of Christmas lights. He tried straining the stress away, but the mess of glyphs and squiggly lines was too much. He tapped at his earpiece, hoping that would fold the goggles up—maybe when they were not so busy.

Suddenly, Fitz's voice roared through the squealing commotion. "I said keep the..."

A shattering explosion of crimpling metal cut his words off in a flash. Gravity came out of nowhere, shoving Damon full tilt into his shoulder harness. He was sure his left shoulder popped out of joint. The whole arm felt numb as a sea of sewing needles.

Damon wiggled his head. His eyes focused on the mess ahead. The dome looked fine by itself. The clutter of tools and bikes, on the other hand, might've been a different story.

Heh! Whoever this garage belonged to better hope they had insurance.

"What is insurance?" Fitz groaned. His eyes quickly shot out of a faint glare. "My apologies. Leave your goggles on, my lord. You'll require them in order to locate the last of the stones."

Damon withdrew his right arm. "Right," he chanted. "Right, sorry. Did I just crash the ship?"

"Indeed," Fitz hummed softly. "I would no doubt suspect your father would be no less displeased than I at this moment."

"Ah, shut up!" Damon growled. Never had he felt his face glow so red. He turned Fitz's way. The worm dog twiddled his cat-like beard like some girly scout guide. So he dropped into in that state of mind again. Damon scoffed. Whatever! He didn't bother talking to a cat who kept switching gender roles like this.

"Now what?" he shot. He paused to clean his fluttery voice. "So you think we should check the damage before anyone...?"

Fitz shot from his chair in a buzz. His eyepiece rolled across the floor, flashing glyphs of amber and red. Damon hadn't noticed those colours reflecting off Fitz's owl eyes before.

"Out!" Fitz cried sharply. "Out quick and fetch the stone!"

"Now what?" Damon repeated in a panting puff. He chased the worm dog out the cockpit, through a scuffle of black octagon cases in the largest of closets, and out the rear hatch. Only as he touched the crimpled mess of Dad's driveway did he realize how many lights have lit up in the neighbourhood.

There was no way anyone could have missed the crashing noise, even this late at night. Any time now, the police would be revving down the street, sirens blaring, and that would mean....

Damon turned back. Yup. Fitz's ship stuck out of Dad's garage like a sore thumb, or rather, a massive ugly collaboration of metallic silver and brass plating. The subtle hue of green from the long ovals for exhaust pipes didn't help either. The neighbours could spot this obvious display of alien stupidity for miles.

So could those Buzzards.

Batteries

Damon found himself scooting across the wreckage of his house, holding out Zack's metal ball like it were some broken compass. He dared not release it. The ball will more than likely shoot through this mess of wood and mangled fabric. Damon would never find it in time to avoid those dreadful blue and red sirens.

The slight tug here and there helped him through the most of this. The creaks and cracks of feeble woodwork stirred the back of his mind. Even as most of the house already collapsed on itself, the very presence of one simple human being could make it sink into the center of the earth for all he knew.

In the distance, the police sirens approached. It took them long enough to respond to the dozen or so 911 calls.

Damon hurried his footing. He reached the kitchen sink, still bare and scratch-free. The basement door shouldn't be far from this mark.

"Here we are," Fitz's voice called.

Damon jumped. The worm dog stood right next to him, holding out that magnet gauntlet of his.

"I thought you were fixing your ship!" Damon cawed.

"The light absorption cells are beyond repair," Fitz sighed. "We would be within luck to reach the fountain before the Buzzards detect the foreign material on the outer hull."

"Foreign material?" Damon shrieked. "How about the rest of the ship? Can it still fly?"

"Yes, yes!" Fitz scowled. "Keep the temper down. That form of impact wouldn't leave the slightest scratch on diamond glass."

Damon's brain quivered. Diamond glass? Hadn't he heard this from somewhere?

"Diamond glass," Fitz continued, "is perhaps the only material that the better half of the Known Galaxy use in constructing anything that require the ability to withstand the vacuum of space. Its strength and durability outmatches all other elements, artificial or otherwise. Its greatest downfall is its weight around larger planets, especially those of a gaseous nature."

Damon drew a stubby nod. Fitz blinked his way.

"Just so you know," lipped the worm dog, "I assumed you wanted to ask."

"You assumed right," Damon nodded. "So, what's the glove for? I thought it work on magnetic metals."

"Correct," Fitz nodded. "There is plenty of it scattered through all the wood."

Damon slapped his forehead. Right! He remembered how Zack would try to find stubs in the wall using his magnetic flashlight. Man, did Mom throw fits every time she saw that flashlight in pieces.

Then the cave scene played out all over again. Piece by piece, Fitz drew slabs of wall and ceiling from the jumbled mess. An opening came about, emerging from the cloud of drywall dust. Damon meant to cover his mouth, but he could hardly breathe with Zack's ball pressed against his mouth. He sucked it up and hacked like a chain smoker.

"Terrible cough you have there," Fitz grunted. Damon changed the subject.

"How much time do I have?"

"As much as you need," Fitz answered. "So long as I'm alive, this glove will prevent any form of collapse."

"Don't get distracted," Damon nodded. He shot into the dark, clambering down the rustic basement stairs like a clattering tin can toy.

The tug of Zack's ball was unbearable. Damon's arms were all pins and needles for cradling the darn thing so tight in his hands. He nearly missed that last step again.

Through that final door and into the old' cellar Damon went. He lurched on like some rusty old monster made of bone and bolts. The power Zack's ball drew could drop an elephant in a hurry. He minded himself not to be that stubborn elephant. He let go, eyes peeled on that faint shot of silver. It vanished beneath the oil tank, exactly as he expected.

"I hear sirens!" Fitz's voice announced from the heavenly hole above. Damon grimaced. Was that worm dog deaf or what?

He dropped to his hands and knees gently. A quick peek of silver flashed on his eyes. Ah, the blue ember glowed like a single hot coal in the midst of a sea of ash. Now, what made it glow like that? What was its power source?

"I see weird flashing lights!" Fitz called. "I think I smell burning rubber, too."

Damon's heart fizzed. Obviously, Dad hadn't taught him much about Earth at all.

Damon bolted back to the stairs. The third one snapped right in half, but he pushed up in the nick of time. He evaded the last one, punching through that miserable cloud of dust. Fitz's figure was up ahead. That drywall stuff had better not give him cancer. He couldn't afford using these stones for that sort of thing.

Damon didn't wait for Fitz's commendation. He upped and ran for that rear hatch. He could hear Fitz pant shortly behind him.

"Good catch."

"Now's not the time," Damon answered in a huff.

"Police! Halt!" cried a crackled megaphone. Damon ignored it. The police officers should've realized now what they were dealing with.

"I said 'Halt!'" cried the megaphone.

"Blow it out your ear!" Fitz snapped back.

Big mistake! Damon hadn't the time to explain. The police officers already had their guns drawn. The way Fitz looked all dazed and confused in the hatch, those officers weren't going to think twice before capping off a warning shot.

KRAKK!

"Don't move!" cried the officer. He aimed his pistol Damon's way.

"In the ship!" Fitz called from the hatch. "They're not going to..."

"Shut it and hit the ground!" called the first officer.

A deathly chill hit Damon like an anvil. He might as well be stuck between a rock and a hard place than right here on Dad's chewed up driveway. His mind fizzled with points of authority. He could feel the rattle of questions squeal in the back of his eyes, blinding him of Fitz's figure standing in front of him. The sight of the police officers and their guns rang clearly in these thoughts.

He turned around like the police officer asked, slowly.

Then he saw the hovering blob of black behind the radio tower hill. Clouds clung to this blob like leeches. That couldn't be a good sign.

"Good!" the first police officer commended. "Now face that big prop of yours and..."

"This is not a prop!" Fitz protested. "Look behind you, you fools!"

"Shut up!" barked the officer. "You, kid. On your knees and hands behind..."

A vibrant explosion cut the officer's voice like a spider's thread. The sky filled with a radiant orange, like the fruit but like nuclear liquid. Damon didn't want to know what had exploded. He made his exit, stage left.

Before he knew it, Damon crammed himself in his cockpit seat. Fitz already had the ship revved up full tilt.

"Keep your hands..."

Damon cut the warning off. "I know! Get us out of here!" He heard a chuckle from Fitz's curled lips.

"Spoken like a true leader in distress." He flicked at the air in front of him.

Dad's garage disappeared in a snap. Only the fork and front wheel of Dad's infamous road bike clung to the dome. Flashes of rabid squirrels squealed through his head. All the bones ached from that mess back on the hill. Or was it the terminal velocity pulsing through the entire ship?

Damon called out to Fitz. He couldn't even hear himself. Yup! That was terminal velocity all right. It was rather cool to feel it first hand, but annoying. For some reason, it made his eyes feel like liquid jelly. He bit his lip hard. The last thing he wanted was for his arms to shoot up to rub his eyes. That might plant this ship in the ground like a pea pod!

Fitz seemed to be fine in his seat, flicking at the air here and there. Whenever he twisted his wrist, clockwise or counter, Damon's stomach rolled that same direction. Whenever the worm dog wobbled his left arm, Damon's stomach would try to jump out of his chest. Thank goodness for that rib cage of his.

All the while, the world before Damon became more of a blur than anything else. He couldn't recognize tree from hill or building from rock cliff. Some rock cliffs emitted an extra gush of jitter in Damon's gut. He tried and watched how Fitz moved around them. But each time he tried, his hand would inch up. He'd quickly reset himself in his seat for good merit. He wasn't about to mess up Fitz's ride at the speed of light.

The blurry lines continued for some time. Finally, Damon's nerves collapsed. He shot his head to Fitz's way.

"What are you doing?"

"Outrunning the Hive ship," Fitz answered. His tone suggested an annoyed grunt somewhere between the lines.

"Well," Damon started. "We have the stones already. Can't we try to latch on the ship or something?"

"Whatever for?"

"Zack!" Damon exclaimed, frustrated. "Zack, you can of worms! We still have to..."

His stomach rolled hard before he could finish. His legs flapped like paper tails in a hurricane clinging for dear life.

Suddenly, the whole screen went blank. Damon couldn't see anything for the longest time. All he could relate to was the hoarse breaths of a fuzzy worm that smelled more like a wet dog dragged in from a swamp.

"Enough of the distractions!" Fitz hollered. "I've enough of your constant whining, human! Just spill out your thoughts right here and now."

"Where are we?" Damon blinked. He could see the blur of the central display lighting up once again.

"A cavern in the Nevada Desert!" Fitz announced coldly. "No bitter tongue, my lord! Only questions and assumptions."

Damon sucked in that last comment. It burst into nothing before he could let his next curious bubble. The fact that his right hand still felt hard and warm might have something to do with it.

"These stones," he started. "No...What exactly are these stones about?" He held out Grandpa's stone and stared cold in its ember. He wished he could hear Grandpa.

"What kind of stone are they?" he said.

"The Elder Stones," Fitz announced. "As much as they bring life to nearly every piece of *mechina* in the Known Galaxy, they are not intended for that purpose. They never have."

"So..." Damon raced for the right words. "What are they worth?"

"The value is indescribable," said Fitz. "There are more than enough of Elder Stones in the Known Galaxy, but few exist for what the Empire has worked them for."

"Okay," Damon chuckled. "Funny how this ember keeps glowing like it does. There's no flicker." He checked all sides on the stone. "No power switches, either. How much energy's in it anyway?"

"Blue is near-infinite," Fitz nodded. "It should generate nearly double the capacity of your planet's energy without ever being replaced."

Damon went to speak up, but Fitz beat him to the draw.

"Mind you," hummed the worm dog, "You will require storing the stone deep beneath the earth behind enough layers of diamond glass to resist the strongest of the Empire's godly hands."

Damon stared. "Hunh?"

Fitz fingered at nothing. "Weapons of immeasurable strength. A five-foot barrier of diamond glass will withstand it, but you would require twice as much..."

"How much does it blow up?" Damon interrupted.

Fitz paused for a while. Damon didn't need to hear the answer to understand.

"Two of your stars would go supernova, side by side," said Fitz. "Even the Illori could not withstand such a force."

"And these stones?" Damon chirped.

Fitz sighed. "They were forged as weapons for our former masters."

Damon let the answer sink in. No wonder Fitz looked so hurt. There must be some real nasty memories buried thick in the worm dog's head.

He glanced at the stone, then to his side, and then to stone. "Weapon, hunh? I take it you suck the souls out of people or something, right?"

Fitz said nothing. His eyes dawned far and beyond.

"It's okay," Damon breathed. "This isn't the first time someone tried to tell me a dirty secret. My grandpa was choked full of them." He paused a moment. "Funny, though. All of that came to this ship...and this stone."

Damon waved the stone gently to the side. "So why suck souls out people, hunh?"

"Don't you point that anywhere near me!" Fitz roared, swinging his gauntlet right for the stone. A blistering force sent Damon's arm all the way around to his right. His hand clenched, perhaps too tight, against the crystal-like surface. He could feel a glyph or two burned into his palm.

"Keep it away from me!" Fitz scowled. "The way you treat them, you'd think they were meant to be throwing stones."

"Well..." Damon moaned. "I guess you could say we humans would rather call these movie props than weapons. Heck! I don't think Area 51 would even blink at this."

Fitz scowled at nothing. "Their stupidity shall be their downfall," he bowed. "Little do you humans realize how close your entire populations—and planet—have been to death. I can account three incidents in which my...the Empire have intervened with the Illori. I, myself, had to sacrifice more than my worth to ensure the last attempt on your planet was the very last."

Damon scratched his head. "Illori?"

"The Illori," Fitz echoed. "My former masters. Be thankful the Empire has wiped the bulk of them from our existence. Had they succeeded in moving beyond the boundaries of good faith, you will not exist. Your father would have no mate to afford in his now retreat."

"She's my mom!" Damon exploded kindly. "Don't you dare talk to her like she's some sort of disposable baby making machine. Do I make myself clear?"

"Absolutely," Fitz nodded with a feeble smile.

Damon smirked. "Batteries full of soul! Ha! Good one, Fitz!" Fitz gave him his Mom's stare. He quickly cleared his throat. "So to speak."

"You mock it for humour," Fitz lipped. "The empress prefers her greed. She seeks power in the most ungodly fashion, breaking the line between the fabrics of our own existence and that of the Illori."

All of those meaningless words came crashing on Damon like an avalanche full of mud. "Say what?"

"Trust me," said Fitz. "You are best not to know."

Damon shrugged. "Fair enough." He gazed at the black in front of him. "So what are we staring at, anyway? Shouldn't we...?"

Fitz bent himself out of whack in that seat of his. "I've already told you," he stated firmly, "we wait in cover of the Nevada caves until the Hive ship passes. And then we shall make our move back..."

"Hold on!" Damon raised his tone sharply. "Nevada, right?"

"Yes," Fitz said slowly. "What of it?"

"You mean Area 51?"

Fitz giggled like a girl scout. "Absolutely no."

Damon crimpled his eyes. "I thought you said..."

"You thought wrong." Fitz grew back in his manly mode again. "Your so-called secret military installment has no connection to the Known Galaxy's historical archives. In their eyes, the Roswell Incident never existed."

"Okay...," Damon fingered.

"No," Fitz answered. "I am responsible for what is referred to as the Tunguska Fireball on your planet. That is the last recorded existence of the Illori in the Known Galaxy. That is the undiluted power of our precious stones."

The name Tunguska stuck itself to the root of Damon's mouth like peanut butter. He had heard that name before in one of his video games...and on that internet encyclopedia of sorts.

Oh, wait!

"Tunguska," he spilled out from his gut. "You mean that Siberian fireball scientists keep banging each others' heads over...." When Fitz didn't answer, Damon pushed on a little more. "That...that..." His voice lost a bit of touch with itself. "Yeah, that fireball that wrecked a good lot of forest back before World War 1. A whole lot of them said it was a comet or a meteor of sorts."

"Of sorts," Fitz grumbled. "Again, your kind is subjected to much stupidity, all because the Empire will not allow anyone to give blessings of knowledge to your leaders."

"Ha!" Damon cried. "If that Bush guy was still in the White House, he'd start shooting missiles at you. Really! Half the world would rather blow you guys up than listen to you. Most of them don't think you ought to exist."

"Religion has its rotten seeds," Fitz sighed.

Damon whistled. "Don't go there," he warned coolly. "They'll grab their pitchforks and shotguns, if you know what I mean."

Fitz rubbed his shoulder gingerly. "Aye. Your father can be quite a..."

He stopped right there, staring as though he'd seen death coming straight for him. Damon could see some sort of amber glyph flashing off Fitz's amber eyes. He reached out, ready to snap his fingers, but word of mouth caught him in the act.

"Back in your seat," Fitz commanded. "We must relocate before the Buzzards..."

A massive rattle filled Damon's body. He almost had to slide off the seat for a toilet seat. How many earthquakes did he have to go through to get to the end?

Fitz threw a few punishable words into the mix. "Spite their terrible tactic at this hour," he cursed. "They are not supposed to use any of their long range weapons on this planet. Not even the empress would allow it, no matter how desperate she is to take you in as a slave."

Fitz's words were more like a paper shredder than a heart massager. Damon could barely keep his gut sunken. He could barely retain his rage.

"I'm supposed to be some stupid slave?" he barked.

"Did you miss all the talk we've exchanged over the past week?" Fitz scowled, his voice full of bitter almonds. "The empress ordered the Buzzards here to obtain you and any siblings under the Enslavement Act. They want to turn you into gladiators for cheap thrill."

"Cheap!" Damon choked. "Are you kidding...?"

He broke off beneath the rattle of a new quake. The rattle echoed deep and thick in his ears. Man, did that feel close or what?

Fitz flicked his finger. A glaring flash swallowed the cockpit whole. Damon whipped off his goggles at once. He strained his eyes as hard as he could, but no matter how hard the sides of his fists rub down, the cream yellow glare could not bleed out from his eyes.

Once again, his stomach rolled left and right, leapt, and tucked. Never did it plug his nose. No, there wouldn't be enough space for that sort of dive the way this ship sped around this planet. Now, if only Damon could read these jerks and jumps, he might figure out what sort of funky trick Fitz pulls off with his rubber arms.

Shades of black cut through the unsightly glare. Damon finally found those shapes and colours he so desperately tried to rub back in. So far, he hadn't heard any complaints from Fitz. Maybe he was too busy to notice what Damon had done.

"Are you going to help?" said a stern voice. It prickled at Damon's neck hair like arctic ice.

"Help with what?" he snorted back.

"The piloting controls!" Fitz snapped. "Are you going to enter in the address to your grandfather's forest? Or am I going to be searching for it all day?"

Damon choked on his pride. "What? Are you crazy?" He wiped spittle from the bridge of his lips. "I don't know Grandpa's address! And even if I did..." A sudden lurch in his gut made him stop for a moment. "Even if I did, I wouldn't tell you. Not with those Buzzards blasting at us with their so-called *illegal* weapons."

"Then what do you suggest?"

"Latch on their ship!" Damon scowled. "Do some funky beanbag trick so they'd think we left town. Then we can hide on their blind spot, get in, snatch Zack and Zoe, get back in, and then get back to that fountain you're so brained out about."

Damon sucked in all that air he let out. Seesh! Since when did he start mouthing orders like a cadet Chief Warrant Officer?

"Back at you!" Fitz snapped.

"What?"

"Your plan," breathed the worm dog. "The failure rate is astronomical, especially this part where we are to transfer ourselves to the Hive ship. The Hive ship has no blind spot. It is a biological vessel, thus is able to detect any and all foreign objects touching it, no matter how hard that leech tries to..."

Fitz broke off. *Just in time, too*, Damon thought. He could see Fitz's owl eyes pound at him with a most ferocious stare. Besides, he still had to pilot this wondrous beast. Damon, too, broke to the sight before him. The ship hovered over a multitude of luscious greens. They were not quite Grandpa's trees but more Amazonian like. Then Fitz's eyes sank in his heart like a pair of lead stones.

"What?" he quirked.

"What in the Ragnorak inspired your petty little plan?" exclaimed the worm dog. His tone took a sharp turn for the better. "Stunner missiles fast approaching. Brace yourself."

"Hunh?"

More spinning and jerking. Now, the horizon was flipping around, spinning like some massive canvas of hilly trees and rock on a mobile canvas. Well, whatever that meant, Damon finally found out how fake those gaming flight simulators have been for the past while.

The rolling stone in Damon's gut came to a stop. He could hear Fitz shoot off his earlobes with a clash of verbal diarrhea.

"Stun missiles," Fitz announced. "They would be best described as low impact projectiles each carrying a detonator and a biotechnological form of electromagnetism. If I try to explain any more, my head will hurt, and you'll be forced to drive."

"Uh..." Damon started. He stopped as he realized his stone was missing from his hands. He scanned the cockpit left and right, but couldn't find a hint of the blue ember.

"Worry about loose objects later," Fitz suggested. "If you don't have your goggles on already, do me a favour. I might require some piloting assistance in case one of the missiles connect."

Damon scanned the floor again. This time, his eyes met with his earpiece so neatly jammed between his feet. He scooped it up and snagged it over his burning lobe. The goggles instantly formed before his eyes, displaying that all too familiar warm up screen of reds and greens.

A sickening string bowed in his gut. He eyed Fitz for the moment it took to ask, "We're not taking the Hive down, are we?"

Fitz did not budge from his focused stare. "If need be," he said. "If not, we can force the Hive ship to land by hiding in the trees once more. Persuading them to actually land, though, will be bothersome."

Damon scowled with all the bitterness he could spare. "You're hopeless!" he announced.

What a miserable jerk this Fitz turned out to be. He probably didn't even have a plan to start out with. No wonder they ran around the globe like they were wearing blindfolds. No wonder they hadn't made their way back to the fountain already.

"Foolish missiles..."

Damon meant to snap something back. A sudden lurch in his gut made him forget.

Then it happened!

A blob of black swallowed the dawn like a plague of mosquitoes. A missile streaked underneath the dome. It jerked up and struck the lightless blob in an instant. Then a ship maybe ten times of this one popped out of nowhere, like the missile hit the cloaking on/off switch.

Cool! Damon thought for that very second his stomach slammed hard against the back of his ribs. He swore he nearly lost his lunch on the spot.

Fitz looked stunned all of the sudden. Did one of those missiles hit him in the gut, too?

"No, no, no..."

The worm dog muttered under his breath as he rattled his arms in place. "What act of foolishness...?" A reeling silence filled the air, and then...

The Hive ship veered like some sick puppy heading straight for a brick wall. It slammed straight across the side of a hill once heavily dotted with trees. A rolling thunder broke through the seams, piercing every inch of the air with a deadly shrill. A plume of flame swallowed much of the air before them.

The first thing to crash into Damon's thoughts came bursting through his lungs and out of his mouth. He couldn't help but shout his brother's name.

The Last Leg

"ZACK!"

"Stay in your seat!" Fitz commanded.

Damon hardly moved an inch. His entire body wanted to explode, and yet he knew. He knew the slightest movement would send them into that hill in every bit the same way.

Still, his heart raged on, slamming against the back of his ribs like a wrecking ball. His lungs fluttered in and out, in and out, without a single grasp for focus. His nails dug deep into the silicon fabric of his armrests. The shoulder restraints bit into him like a pair of rabid claws. He couldn't sit there and watch that fireball light up the forest, and yet....

And yet....

He couldn't move. It wasn't out of Fitz's demands. It was his stomach! It pulled him back in his seat. It warned him against flying full front into a train wreck.

Fitz seemed to notice. Every time Damon blinked, Fitz would flick his arms. It almost looked impulsive, and yet the way the worm dog chewed on his bloodied lip....

"Stop thinking!" Fitz commanded, stern as ever. "I must find a reasonable altitude to assess the situation..."

Damon exploded. "ASSESS THE SITUATION? THE WHOLE SHIP'S BLOWN UP, YOU IDIOT! ZACK'S DEAD!"

"He is *not* dead, my lord!"

Damon couldn't believe what he heard. How could anyone survive that crash? "Oh, yeah?" he spat in Fitz's direction. "Then what was that? A..."

Fitz cut him off. "Now's not the time to be sarcastic about the matter. An event occurred within the Hive Ship before it overrode its own offensive tactics."

"What?" Damon snapped. "You mean they all went mutiny at each other? Ha! That's a story and a half. If you ask me, Fitz, you've been watching too many Hollywood movies."

Fitz lifted a corner of his short-lipped mouth. "In a manner of speaking, it is not this Hollywood as you claim. Now, keep seated and pay attention. I'm going to show you how we are to conduct..."

SMAT!

The dome fluttered with an agonizing yellow. Damon shrieked. The stiffening sound of glass crunching raked through his brittle ears. He stomached the obvious—a Buzzard clinging to the front of the ship.

"Get us out of here!" Damon bellowed impulsively. The ship didn't move.

"Fitz!"

Nothing came of the fuzzy creature. Damon scowled at the worm dog. Fitz didn't move. He sat frozen in his chair like some ghost sucked out his soul. His eyes favoured a hint of violet for some reason.

Crunch! Crunch!

The Buzzard continued poking at the dome with its razor steep claws. Damon thought up a giant fly swatter, but his imagination couldn't move past his eyes. The Buzzard—it simply smiled back at him with its six eyes and its pine needle teeth. Damon gasped for dead air. He had to get this thing off the ship somehow.

Flick the arms....

Damon reefed his neck up. "Fitz?" he called in the midst of the Buzzard's poisonous shadow.

Flick the arms, a faint voice simmered from afar. Damon swore it came from outside the ship, but seeing how it was supposed to be made out of some impossible metal, that would be impossible as well.

"Fitz, where are you?" Damon stammered. He restrained his arms to their appropriate rests. He would not allow himself to crash this ship. His ears twitched. Was that the vent blowing in his ear?

The ship cannot be damaged by your ploy, said the wind current. *Flick your arms in the right direction. It should follow your heart as it has done mine.*

Damon jumped to the matter. He shoved his left arm into the fray, snapping his fingers forth like a rock star. The ship sprung to life, its forward projector slamming the Buzzard against the cracked dome.

But torque wasn't enough to dislodge the bug on the windowsill. Damon didn't need to look far for a pair of wiper. The trees could do that.

He steadied his arms out before him. The ship rattled then nothing more. *Good,* Damon thought. He knew how to roll the ship—that twisted the wrist. But to pitch was a whole different thing. He tried lowering his hands down, but the ship simply spun on the spot. No, that was the body. The engines must have a different way of interpreting themselves.

So why was Fitz snapping his fingers all over the place? What exactly was he looking at that made the ship steer so well?

Damon eyed a tree beyond the Buzzard's left flank. He reached out to shove the Buzzard out of the way.

"Woah!"

The ship sped forward like a bat off a baseball. He cringed at himself. The Buzzard was on the other side!

He pulled back his hands. His stomach shoved straight into his heart. The Buzzard didn't look impressed. It dangled from the right hand. A quick blink and Damon realized it was missing claws from the other. The claws still embedded themselves in the dome glass. Damon was going to really have to scrape that windshield clean. He tried flicking at the Buzzard. The ship moved not an inch. Okay, how about that tree over....

Before Damon could wave his arm, the ship jumped into blinding speed. It ploughed through a clutter of maple and beech like they were nothing. Damon tried waving his arms, but a sudden force threw them out of his goggle's sight. Limb after tree after rock smashed across the dome on either side, bringing those slight chips into full-blown cracks.

Still, the Buzzard kept hold. Everything missed by either a hand span, or maybe by a scratch. Damon couldn't see in front of him. He could not snap his fingers where his goggles couldn't....

Wait a sec. The goggles could map the terrain? Was that how Fitz flew the ship this whole time?

Damon tried a snap for the sky. The ship spat out of the forest like a wad of spit. He tried a combo at the first crack of sunlight—a wave of his right arm and the twist of his left wrist. The ship turned itself around. Not completely but enough for the inside of Damon's stomach to boil. Seesh! He had forgotten about his fear of heights.

Still, the ship sped on upwards. The trees no longer looked like those plastic models on Dad's old RPG battle sets. They looked more like dots off a computer screen. The Buzzard let out a retching grin. Its teeth stirred Damon's heart like chopsticks. How it could resist such tremendous speeds was beyond Damon in another universe....

Maybe.

Damon held his breath and snapped a figure. The ship plummeted at such a speed that his eyes filled with stars. His whole insides felt like they've been flattened against his spine. The scenery grew closer and closer until he could see the leaves on the trees. His brain could have used a little tuning. Man, did it ever feel like he had a bloody nose....

THUNK!

All of gravity snagged Damon in his shoulder restraints. One popped, maybe out of joint. Damon couldn't tell. For some reason, his body didn't feel like letting out any pain.

He let out his breath. One by one, his shallow rasps shed the stars away. The looming darkness from the ground straight in front of him blanketed him in fear. He tried not closing his eyes, and yet, he felt that tingling feeling that time completely stopped.

Was he going to die?

A scraping noise flickered throughout the cockpit. Damon blinked. He barely noticed the Buzzard's shadow blobbing about in front of him. After a descent like that, how could it still be alive?

"Get off the ship already!" he hollered. The Buzzard simply scratched on the dome. Surely, it must be dazed. Otherwise, there'd be more than those cracks in the dome right now.

Still, it clung to the windshield. Damon was no closer to....

THUMP!

Damon held his breath. What was that?

More thumping shook the cockpit. All of them felt distant, like they were on the back of the ship.

Aw, crap! They were after the rear hatch!

Damon shot out his hands and arms. Twist after wave, he got the ship level with the ground. A quick snap here and there shot him through the trees. Finally, a limb came out and cracked the bug right off the dome. It left a pretty good crack on the glass, too.

Wait a sec! What happened to the claws and those other cracks? They upped and vanished, too! Damon gasped. Now, what kind of glass was this?

The thumping from the back of the ship worsened. Damon tipped the back of the ship down. It rattled and it groaned. *Good*, Damon thought. He must be dragging the backside like a dog would. A mass of squealing followed. He waved a salute to the cockpit hatch. Goodbye, fleas.

Damon counted to five. Then he lifted the rear up and snapped at the sky. The ship lifted at blistering speed. A twist of the wrist and another snap threw the ship back toward the ground. Damon slapped his hand across, and all that rush to his head stopped. Many thumps and bangs rattled the ship for several seconds. Then one by one, the Buzzards Damon claimed toppled to the earth.

A quick peek across the terrain brought a smile over Damon's fears. He snapped at a groove not far from the south of the fountain hill. He pulled out his mic piece and called, "Land here." A short jolt later, the goggles retreated into Damon's earpiece. He pulled it off his boiling lobe slow and gentle.

In that moment of sharp breaths and exploding heartbeats, Damon managed to squeeze three words from his mouth.

"That...was...awesome..."

He expected some sarcastic remark in the dusk of the action, but none came.

"Fitz?" Damon called. "You okay?"

Nothing.

Damon pulled his shoulder straps off. Ink drops tethered his fingertips. His shirt had been torn where the straps bit in. Weird, though. With the bloodstains, he'd usually find pain and at least part of the wounds, but not this time. His skin had completely stitched itself, and it wasn't from the stone.

He shook it out of his head. "Fitz!" Still, there came no answer. Damon reached over. He could barely see the worm dog in this miserable light. The ship faced the wrong way to let in the sun from this angle. He needed to shed light from somewhere else.

What about the old fossil? What did Fitz call it again? Elf stone or something? Again, Damon shook the clatter from his head. He reached over the lip of the floor and snagged the stone. A gentle blue haze billowed from the ember, engulfing the cockpit in a hypnotic haze.

For a moment, Damon felt like wrapping himself in a blanket. He felt like taking himself to the nearest couch, preferably....

Fitz sprung to life in a frenzy of deep, crackling coughs. Damon shook away his disjointed thoughts. He stuffed the stone in his pocket and reached for the worm dog's shoulders. A good shake ought to clear away the smoke.

"Fitz!" he called. "Fitz, snap out of it!"

The worm dog muttered something.

"Eh? What?" said Damon.

Fitz slapped his arms away. "Refrain from touching me with your frigid hands." His coughing fit died in a snap. "My body lies cold as it is."

Damon crimped up a frown. "What? These seats don't have heat pads in them? Fitz! Even the dome heals itself. It's like this ship's got a ticking heartbeat or something." He fluttered his eyes feverishly. What did he say?

"These seats..." Fitz began, only to break off. His head rolled gently across the back of his seat. The muscles in his neck twitched here and there. His nails seemed stiff against the armrests. Confusion mixed itself like cement in that bucket called Damon's brain.

"Are you okay?"

Fitz unbuckled and rolled himself from his seat. His big left hand missed the ground completely. Damon had to jump in to save him from a bitter fall.

"Thank you," Fitz bowed feebly.

"No problem," Damon nodded back. "And really, are you okay?" He meant it from the bottom of his heart.

"No," Fitz sighed. "I believe I've been poisoned by projectiles." He hacked up a lung and some neon orange snot with it.

Damon's stomach began to curdle. "Projectiles? Fitz, that bug..."

"Buzzard."

"That Buzzard..." Damon paused to gesture at the dome. "Nothing came through. They probably shot at us a dozen times when they latched on, but nothing came through."

"I have already warned you," Fitz sighed. "The Buzzards have no interest in harming you beyond the need to capture you for enslavement. They require poison only as a last resort to assassinate someone."

"Fitz," Damon gritted. "You're not getting it. Nothing...." He blinked at the dribble of dark syrup from Fitz's mouth. A memory turned on in the back of his head. A good mess of it splattered in his eyes when Dad shot at him....

Wait a sec! That was not chocolate syrup. That was blood! Alien blood! Damon swatted his forehead. How could he be so stupid?

"Rock salt," he grimaced. "Fitz, it's only rock salt. And from the looks of those scars on your back, I'd say you've been a meat grinder at one point."

Fitz chuckled—a manly chuckle, thank goodness. "Believe me, my lord. If my body could tolerate salt in the manner that you do, I would have handled your father without your interference."

Damon curled his lips. "So you're allergic to salt, eh?"

Fitz shut his eyes for maybe half a minute. "I suppose that would be the appropriate conclusion. I, for the life of my gods, cannot understand why I failed to reach such conclusion before."

He led Damon into the back of the ship, limping like a broken dog. Damon didn't realize until now how much brown blood leaked from the worm dog's left shoulder. Half his front leg was saturated with it.

"And it still hasn't healed!" Fitz growled as he shifted through the nearest set of drawers. "Now where did I stash the mineral solution?"

"That's probably loaded with salt, too," Damon warned wearily. "Try that herbal stuff you used on me."

"You depleted our supply last eve."

"Okay...."

Damon couldn't help but stare at the rear hatch. He made his approach, fingers reaching out to brush against the cold metallic gloss. The bitter sounds of Fitz fussing through the closets for some magic alien remedy passed along the back of Damon's head.

In all the mess that Damon dragged the ship through, he couldn't find a single dent or scratch. Sure, he'd like to swing a bat into this stuff. Let's see how quick it'd take to dent his bat.

Oh, wait! He didn't have his bat.

"Found it!"

Damon withdrew from the door. He turned to Fitz with an eye half cocked beneath its droopy brow. Fitz stood half-erect over a tangle of familiar household items. But of all the things Fitz would pull out, who would think of that? Especially with all that mucky brown stuff sticking to the bristles?

"What's that all about?"

Fitz clipped his shoulder gauntlets from his mail suit. "A firm form of cleaning my wounds," said the worm dog.

"That's a toilet brush," Damon irked. His stomach was about to blow. Only to see a toilet brush with mucky brown stuff....

Fitz raised the brush momentarily. "I assure," he said coolly. "It is my blood. And yes, it is the only way I am to brush away the remnants of your father's actions from my wound."

Damon steered back to the rear hatch. "Fine, fine!" he burped. "How about telling me how to open this hatch, eh? I'll see if I can find some way back to the shipwreck." He heard what sounded like Fitz's mail suit rolling on the floor. Or was that a piggy bank full of loose change?

"You are not required to save your brother," Fitz noted. Damon could hear that toilet brush scrub. Ooh, how that disgusting sound makes his shoulders shiver. He dared himself never to look back—never to see Fitz and that bloodstained toilet brush.

"I can't help it," Damon confessed. "I have to know if he's still alive."

"He is."

Damon broke his dare. He spun around and looked Fitz hard in the eyes. "What kind of telepathy are we talking here anyway?"

Fitz set the toilet brush aside. "None, really. I have taught your brother many of the needs to escape such a situation. In fact, I have no doubt he is climbing the fountain hill at this very moment. Now, if only..."

Damon stopped the worm dog there. "I need to be up that hill, Fitz. I need to be up there with everything we have. I need to know how that fountain works, okay?"

"Patience," Fitz nodded as he poked at the crater in his shoulder. "You will be safer at the fountain than you are here, but in between, the Buzzards will no doubt try to capture you in any means they can muster." The worm dog reached out a hand dripping with alien blood. "Now, if you don't mind..."

Damon hesitated. He bit his lip and dug in his pocket. Out went the stone, straight into Fitz's waiting hand.

Then it caught him. A glitter at the edge of his throbbing eyes. Damon stepped up to the plate, wondering how weird karma can get. Yeah, it could, for sure.

"Whose is this?"

Fitz lifted the better of his owl eyes. "Eh?" He spoke in the best Canuck accent Damon had ever heard.

Damon pointed to and picked up the stubby aluminum bat. "Whose is this?" he repeated, caressing the weight of the bat into his arms. Man, did this feel like home all of a sudden.

"The bat?" said Fitz. "Yes, I believe your father handed it to me several moons ago. I can vaguely remember your father's words. Something to do with..."

Damon cut him off. The less he heard of Dad, the better he could pull through this mess of family secrets.

"That's fine," he announced somberly. "I think I'll take a crack at the fountain, then."

"A crack," Fitz smirked. "Ah, I see the pun."

Damon blinked. "Okay."

Fitz withdrew. "My apologies, my lord. There has been the odd night when your...." He crushed his face in like he tasted the mother of potent lemons. "When I was invited to the local dwelling for what you would call TV time. Friends..."

"Call him Dan," Damon grunted.

"Dan," Fitz sighed, his body giving a little shake. "Dan and your mother would teach me puns and parodies of Terra Tetris. Some were vulgar, I assure you. Others simply led to more pronounced...." He paused again. "Well, let's say your father wished to follow through with some commitments we've arranged prior to your...."

Damon piped up the stop sign. "Okay, I think that's enough," he gasped sharply. "Fitz, could you put that shoulder of yours aside and unlatch the back door? I'm kind of itching to get to that fountain before the Buzzards think too much."

Fitz waved a hand, his magnet gauntlet hand. A device shouts out from the ceiling and right into one of his stubby hands. It looked more like a teardrop made of hard silicon or something. Damon would never forget that bluish tint.

The worm dog aimed for the hatch. Damon stepped out of the way.

"A remote, eh?"

Cha-click!

The hatch flung open in a snap. A wave of hot air crackled in Damon's face. He had to shut his eyes.

"The flames are becoming intense," Fitz hummed. "I do not believe the air is quite favourable, either."

"Gas mask?" said Damon. Fitz shook his head. "Then I might as well take off, then." He tipped his bat for Fitz. "See you soon."

Fitz nodded brightly. "Count on it."

Slash and Burn

Damon didn't look back for the slightest mosquito. The Buzzards were big enough to set half the forest on the run. Who wouldn't hear the buzz of their monstrous wings? He sure could, and he had hardly made it past the quarter mark.

It had taken him hardly a peek past the first clearing of wool grass some fifty meters back that brought Damon under a thick haze of regret. He had landed the ship too soon, too far from the base of the fountain hill. Maybe this clearing would have worked, or that trench straight ahead, where he dragged the thrusters through the earth like a dog clearing an itch.

No, the Buzzards would've been on him already. He could see them buzzing about here and there, looking down with their oblong headsets. He'd break behind a decent rock or beneath a good old rot log to be on that safe side.

He remembered how Fitz started rambling on about how the Buzzards could only use certain surface scanners. "It's the way their eyes work," the worm dog explained as he tapped his left eye. "They can detect more forms of light and radiation than any other species. It is perhaps the most prominent reason the Illori had abandoned them to the Empire too quickly. They're too crafty in stealth and heat motion, and yet they could never identify the slightest of intelligent life unless they were looking directly at one.

"That is how they haven't been able to detect us so far. And yes, that is how you managed to evade the pair at the river. They could see your presence clearly, but not your movement."

"Ah," Damon recalled nodding. "The opposite of colour blind."

"Yes, and no," Fitz sighed. "Bah! It is but too difficult to explain the matter without growing worrisome. Hurry to the fountain at once. The barrier should protect your presence there."

Damon didn't think twice to ask questions. He hurried out, baseball bat in hand.

And now, with the buzz of the Buzzards closing in, Damon wished he'd stayed long enough for one more question.

What if they broke past such a wild handicap?

Damon avoided the trench like the plague. Sure, his stomach was screaming for food. The sun peeked about a third way up the sky and not a single marinated pork roast in sight. But it would have to do.

The scatter of many trampled feet rattled the forest, even in the tiniest cracks of the trees. No longer did that deep buzz of insect wings rip through Damon's ears. No doubt, they had spotted him enough times. Now, they're probably trying a way to corner him.

KRAKK!

A tree trunk exploded to the right. Damon ducked and rolled, hammering out a sweat and a sprint. The many snaps and cracks of falling trees crashed all behind him. He thought he heard a faint music tube whistle somewhere in there.

KRAKK!

More tree splinters burst at his face. He pushed his luck, rolled on without ever looking back. Whatever those Buzzards used, he was not going to think an instant....

Another music whistle flashed past his right ear. A golden blur buzzed right past his head, turning briefly into a prickly ring, and then straight back for him. He shoved his feet forward, forced himself into a back summersault. With a decent shove, he spun himself about, baseball bat at the ready. He batted the next ring back to its sender.

One down, infinity to go.

Damon counted the seconds as he scurried through the trees. He lost count the most his foot snagged a gnarly root. A roll and a shove brought him back to count and to a more pleasant haste. Not so much cutting as he hopped here and there.

Another snag. Another trip. Ooh, this drove Damon nuts! How could anyone run through these forests like this? They'd be lucky or plain stunt actors to do this sort of thing! But then, Hollywood was all about stunt acting anyway.

Damon's ears caught a distant rolling thunder. A tree fell somewhere to the west, then another to the truest east and one probably a hundred meters ahead.

Damon hacked out a lung. Oh, great! Now these Buzzards were cutting through the lot like rabid blind wolves! No wonder. The smoke from their ship had probably blinded their scanners altogether. If Damon didn't push himself, he would be fighting with the same handicap—blind as a bat, as one comic vigilante would quote.

He pushed on. He made himself push, no matter how many trees these bugs snapped down. Every fifth step or so, he'd peek up, hoping to find a clearing through all this sweltering heat. Oh, man! The crackling flames came awfully close.

Alas, a break in the smoke brought Damon's eyes up once more. The tip of the mountain's obelisk stuck out of the trees like a sore thumb. His body shivered with thrill. To be this close already?

"Aaaaah!"

Damon jerked to the right. That all too familiar yelp caught his ears on his worst step. He ate dirt and spat the grains through his bloodied lips. The stinging couldn't have set him off any more.

"Zack!" he belted, only to spit more of that grain. "Zack, I'm coming!" He rushed head on into the smoke, bat raised.

More whistles shrieked through the air. Damon swung low. He averted the first one. A second came closer to his head. He belted it into a nearby tree.

A third? Again, Damon swung and hit.

"Aw, come on!" he roared into the mist. Can't you do any...?"

A rabid crunch to the gut left him breathless. He staggered back, both hands clenching his gut. The glitter of his baseball bat left him in the deep haze. Another whistle came for him. He dropped to his knees. The ring sped over his head, narrowly brushing the longest strains of his fuzzy head.

Two more whistles screamed right for him. Their menace removed all hope for a tuck and roll. His gut felt like he'd been hit by an eighteen-wheeler.

"Damon, duck!"

Something dropped him into his side as the two rings clanged into each other. Suddenly, he felt his body dragged through dirt and ash. That familiar grab at the shoulder had his gut reeling for an exit. He held it in, tight and long.

The dragging stopped. Zack's voice shouted from somewhere in the fog. "Come on, you jerk!" he cried in his ranting cry. "Get off your lazy butt and move!"

Damon ripped back. "Can't you see I'm hurt, Zack? Where's my bat? I'm going to smoke the sucker who hit me!"

"There's too much smoke for that!" cried Zack.

Damon let loose a chuckle. He looked his brother in the eye and said, "Nice pun."

"I'm serious!" Zack belted his fury with red. "Zoe's waiting for us there."

"Zoe?" Damon's heart fluttered aloud. Of all the people he forgot in all this mess, it happened to be Zack's one-on-one worker.

He drove his feet into the earth and pushed up. Step by step, he marched his way after Zack into those thorn bushes and out into....

The utter calm.

Damon stood center for a moment, dazed and confused. Three steps back, he would've been gulping fiery smoke into his lungs. But here, everything looked as peaceful as ever, not a puff of smoke in sight.

A butterfly swished ahead of his nose. The air felt fresher than what Damon could remember. He couldn't remember the air feeling this fresh on his strolls with Grandpa all those years ago. In fact, it was like breathing that experience of travelling up one of Alberta's summit lookouts, where one could see the peaks of many mountains for kilometers on end.

Then those annoying fingers of Zack popped right up, inches from Damon's face. Snap after snap after annoying snap.

"Snap out of it, you dolt!" Zack ached. "Where's Mister Fuzzy?"

Damon belted a confused stare. "Mister who?"

Zack looked unimpressed. "Mister Fuzzy, you moron! You know, the guy who saved your butt a few times?"

"Oh," Damon scratched his head. "Fitz."

"Mister Fuzzy!" Zack insisted, teeth bared. Damon shook his head. Why did he even bother with this brat?

"All right," Damon sighed, loosening his rucksack from his shoulders. "I have them here. Hold your pants on."

Zack glared an arctic stare. "My pants are ripped, loser!"

"Enough with the name calling already!" called a voice from the fountain. Only then did Damon notice Zoe perched at the ledge like a humble raven.

"Hello, Damon."

Damon lifted a cheek. "Hi." A blunt jab strafed his knee.

"Will you cut that out?" Zack hollered. "It's bad enough that Dad took off."

Damon stared coldly in the brat's eyes. "And how do you know all of this?"

"Uh..." Zack stared like Damon was supposed to know. "Mister Fuzzy told us?"

Damon blinked. "Fitz?" he hiccupped. "How'd he get to you first?"

Zack flapped his tongue. "Well, he's better than you, duh!"

"Good enough," Damon whistled. "Why isn't he here with you, then?"

Zack shrugged. "You tell me, dork! Now, how about coughing those stones already?"

Damon shook his head. "Real mature, Zachary."

"My name is Zack, you..."

"One more name," Zoe called from the fountain, "and I'll give you a restraint to remember, buster. So shut your lip and hand over the stones."

Zack shriveled up into a cry baby. "Okay..."

Damon nodded, his lower lip puffed. "Impressive."

Zoe lifted her arms. "Not my fault he's like that. The way he tried to hide behind everything getting here, I'd say they beat him up pretty bad."

"Really?" said Damon. "I don't see a single bruise."

Zoe shrugged. "Medicine? Who knows with all these aliens popping out of the woodwork? Nice to see you've pulled through."

"I had help," Damon noted, tossing the rucksack over. "Can't see how he'd beat me to you guys, though. I was sure he'd take a bit with his..." Dared he say it? "His healing tactics."

Zack gave him an odd look. "You mean his toilet brush, right?"

Damon shot a glance at Zoe. The raven had become a ghost in record time.

Zack crimpled back in his cry baby pose. He must've noticed something in her Damon didn't. He took his brother by the collar and pulled him up. Honestly, the rattling in this kid could tumble the CN Tower to dust.

"What is wrong with you?"

Zack puffed a bitter wind. "Honey..."

Damon crimped his face tight. "What?"

"Honey!" Zack barked. "Don't you ever put honey on my sandwich again, okay? Really, it's umber gross what those bees do."

"Oh-kay," Damon answered slowly. "So what did they...?"

"Not telling!" Zack lipped. He crossed his arms and jerked his head away. Little jitters of cursive meanings blew out of his mouth. Damon ignored them, his eyes leaning for Zoe. She dropped back in her raven self.

The raven stood over the lip of the fountain, her feet cemented like glue. In one hand, she carried Damon's rucksack. In the other, a gentle blue light seeped through her fingers. A slight detour from the raven revealed a stone already placed on the obelisk.

"Don't bother," Zoe winded. "He'll babble on about some oversized bee dressed in a pharaoh costume squirting honey at him..."

"BLEAGH!"

Bits of wet dribbled along Damon's leg. Zack bent at the gut, coughing and spitting a foot away. Underneath, a pile of chunky goo singed the grass. Damon quietly stepped away.

"See what I mean?" Zoe gestured as she slipped in the third stone. "Back on that bug ship of theirs? He acted up the whole time. Coughing here, spitting boogers there. All while I've been busy trying to find a way out." She moved to the last stone. "Really. It's like they made him Pharaoh Scaredy Cat in a day."

Damon blinked. His gut began thumping on his brain. Something felt fishy.

"Okay. So what did happen?"

Zoe pulled that last stone to her side. She spun around and perched herself on the lip like that marvelous raven of before. Her eyes glimmered like that deep purple he'd seen in Fitz a little ways back. Her face looked kind of sunken in, too. When did she eat anything last?

"If you want to know," Zoe sighed, "I can't remember anything after your mother put me in my car. She told me to drive off somewhere. Everything blanks out like that."

She mimicked her words by waving flat palms in the air before her. Her eyes seemed zoned out for a moment. Then a blink sent them back to Damon.

"Then I wake up all wet from some sort of sticky goo." Here, Zack began coughing again. Zoe ignored him. "No clothes, no nothing," she said. "Zack's not far from me, pushing one button right after the next. I think he was trying to pull me loose from my cell.

"I took a moment, checked out the room. Looked like a circle of canisters. Most of them were empty. Some had those bug things floating in that stick..." More of that coughing fit broke her right off. "Will you stop that, Zack?"

Zack went silent.

"Anyway," Zoe sighed. "Eventually, Zack did find that button. Let me out. Yadda, yadda, yadda. Took a little bit to wipe off the guck from my body. Zack, of course, couldn't stop staring at me. I told him to fetch some clothes. Had to actually slap him, too."

"Those bugs weirded me out!" Zack retorted.

"No such word," Damon corrected. "Let Zoe talk, okay?"

"Yeah, yeah..."

Damon turned back to Zoe. "So you found some clothes..." He tapered off, scanning the dark leather suit biting Zoe's body. Or was it silicon?

"Yes," Zoe finally smiled. "You like it?"

"A lot," Damon nodded. "So you were saying?"

"Yes," said Zoe. "As it turns out, Zack figured we were in some spaceship of sort. I think he recognized some of the structure in the corridors, and how all these flashy panels at the doors and t-junctions looked."

Zack flared, fist shaking. "I looked out the window, stupid!"

"Honey!" Zoe shot back. That one word sent Zack into another coughing fit. Damon couldn't help but chuckle.

"Anyhow," Zoe sighed, "It didn't take long for us to figure the ship was still around here, right? So we'd have to find some way off. Of course, Zack didn't know where—don't make me say that word—Zack didn't know where on Earth we'd be, and you know how that is."

"Sure," Damon shrugged. "Mountains, deserts, a whole lot of ocean."

"Cities, too," Zoe added. "But I figured, as long as we're close to somewhere where some would notice, we wouldn't have to fend for ourselves.

"Then the blue lights went on. That gave me this headache. Zack thought it was some sort of party, but I knew better. Blue and vomit yellow don't mix well."

"True," Damon nodded, his stomach tugging at his spleen.

"So, Zack checks it out, and what do we get? Some weird stuff going on. Really weird stuff. I mean, my stomach was twisting all over the place, and Zack's hollering and hooting like he's on some sort of roller coaster ride."

"You probably were," Damon smirked. "They were chasing us before the crash."

Zoe's face lifted for a split second. "Oh, yeah," she croaked. "That. Really, Damon, I don't know..."

Damon understood. "Someone steered the ship into one of its own missiles." A pause of thought brought him to a higher sense of gravity. "You didn't happen to get hit by a black out before the impact, did you?"

"Ha!" Zack blurted. "Told you he'd guess that part!"

"Honey!" Damon announced. Zack jumped back to his coughing fit.

"Yup," Zoe went on. "Stuffed Zack in an elevator as we started feeling that sick tug in our stomachs. Good thinking, too. We landed somewhere on the wrong side of the river. The ship must've broken up really good when it hit the hill. We couldn't even recognize it after we pried our way out of our little capsule."

"Oh," Damon cued. "That's how Fitz got to you first. He probably took the other way around the hill."

Zoe nodded. "He told us to put the stones in, but not the metallic orb. Not until he shows up, anyway." With that, she locked the last of the four stones into place.

Damon reached into his pocket. Of course, the ball was still there, waiting for some sort of lock.

"Hey!" Zack spat. "That's mine!"

Damon swiped the stone back to his pocket. "I don't think so, Zack. The ball's our way out of here."

Zack growled. "What? We're going after Dad?"

"I am," Damon announced. "You're going somewhere safe until I sort our family back in place."

Zack seemed to absorb Damon's words like a bitter sponge. His eyes grew wide, but his mouth didn't move.

A sharp whistle caught Damon's lobes. "Over there," said Zoe.

First, he turned to her. Then he followed her pointing arm to a jittery thorn brush, not quite the same as the one Zack pulled him through. A figure lurched out of the brushes, full of eyes and comb teeth. Its glittering armour flashed like that of an Egyptian god.

A Buzzard had made its way in somehow. It drooped forward, two of its legs either broken or twisted. It held up the only limb that looked undaunted. In its hand was a familiar object, dented and scratched beyond belief.

The Buzzard looked straight at Damon. "I trust that this belongs to you."

The Fountain's Wake

Damon reached for his pocket, eyes still glued on the wretched beast. "Zoe!" he called. He let Zack's ball loose with his throwing hand.

His good throwing hand.

A glimmer of light and a whizzing crack blistered the air. Damon lost track of the ball, but he could clearly see his baseball bat lying perfectly still, between him and Zoe. He shot a glance at the Buzzard. The Buzzard bowed, his face twisted in a poisonous smile.

"Nice toss," Damon gestured as the Buzzard limped for him. "Maybe you ought to try out for the Jays. They could use someone of your..."

"Shut the sarcasm!" roared the Buzzard. It lunged forward with the mightiest, clumsiest swing Damon could ever dodge. He plucked the Buzzard's stomach with a light hook—not too hard. This beast hardly had any strength left from its previous battle.

The Buzzard wailed an unearthly groan. Damon rolled off to his left as it dropped forward. His feet never touched the ground.

A reeling bunt drove him hard into the fountain's lip. His face hit the water first before the rest of his body curled underneath. The momentum drew him back, flat against his back. Looking back, he could see one of the Buzzard's twisted legs pointing straight for him. Heh! The Buzzard had still got a bit in him.

"Do not underestimate me," growled the Buzzard, its voice still curiously dark. Damon's ears weren't meant to tell the difference between a man bug and a lady bug.

"I'll do my best," Damon called back, sticking out his tongue. Maybe, if he could rouse this beast's anger a bit, he could find whatever weak point it had and drive it down to the bitter ground.

The Buzzard stood there, laughing. Neither Zack or Zoe would move. The fear in Zack's eyes and the hesitation in Zoe's twitches. They had dealt with this one before.

Damon tossed over a question. "What's your name?" The Buzzard didn't answer. Damon tossed a second. "How about this slave stuff?"

"This is personal business now!" shrieked the Buzzard. "I will not be intimidated by the likes of your kind. My ship. My people...." He gripped on a handle sticking from its back. "My brother."

Oh, great! Damon thought, rolling his eyes, not another one of those nutcases.

"How about I get my bat first?"

"No need," sneered the Buzzard. "None of your bloodline is responsible for my embarrassment. I never cared for the empress' orders anyway."

Damon scowled. "Then stop...."

"HER!" barked the Buzzard. His good arm reached for Zoe. "Her miserable kind did this to me. I would not have lost control of my brother's ship. I would not have lost my brother..."

"Yeah, yeah!" Damon shivered. "Why don't you save your monologues for later, eh? I've still got a bone to pick..."

The Buzzard leapt full tilt at the fountain. Damon jumped to his feet too late. The Buzzard already had one hand yanking at Zoe's collar. She kicked at it, but her feet bounced off its golden striped armour.

Damon threw himself at the Buzzard, once again slipping out of thought. Only when it hit him did he realize the Buzzard still had enough feet to counteract a good backlash. He hit a bushel of fiery leaves before he could blink. A subtle roll out of the thorns drew a meaty sigh—too meaty for a decent recovery. That Buzzard's kick winded him good.

Zoe's screams continued. Zack still won't move. Whatever this bug did to him, it must've made Mom look like the good parent all of a sudden.

"I will tear you apart!" screamed the Buzzard. "I swear on my brother's blood!"

"Let go of me!" Zoe spat back. Damon heard a poisonous wail fling through the air. He looked up in time to watch the Buzzard buckle back. Zoe leapt off the fountain, past the marble tiles. She retreated for the forest, only to stand dead still.

Damon's bat was only about an arm and a foot away from her feet. If he had the wind to shout, he'd have her pass that bat to him. Somehow, this gasping and wheezing wasn't working in his favour.

Fitz hopped out of the brushes, his fur clumpy and drizzled with yellow guck. He looked like he'd been hit by a nuclear bomb, and yet, his stagger carried nothing more than the faint limp of his left front leg.

"More freaks!" Zoe belted, racing for the bat. Damon tried to warn her away, but his voice scratched his throat to shreds.

Fitz raised his magnet gauntlet at chest level. "There shall be no need for that." With a twist, he sent the baseball bat reeling out of Zoe's hand and right at the Buzzard. The Buzzard simply batted the bat out of harm's way. His armbands must have some kind of repulsion system like Fitz's gauntlet.

"You think that can distract me, filth?" scowled the Buzzard.

With that, Fitz simply replied, "Not in the slightest." He squished his magnet hand into a brutal fist. The Buzzard lunged at Fitz, arms and feet wailing. Its poisoning screaming punched at Damon's eardrums. Any louder and his head would pop.

The Buzzard's wailing stopped cold as death. It hovered before Fitz, chest facing down. Its face swelled with hate. Damon would see Grandpa's dead body somewhere in the ebony of those buggy eyes. He'd seen three where he should've seen six. "Impossible!" it spat, swinging its good fist at Sybon. Damon realized, as the fist fell short of its target with every swing, there was no metal on that arm.

Fitz grinned a menacing smile. Half his lower lip swelled a tedious black. "I have all the reasons to toy with you, Sybon," he said. "All that precious metal. I could twist your body and squeeze it like a lemon. I could reshape anyhow I please. And yet, here I stand in a Utopia set upon a hill of toxic fire. I wonder, Sybon....

"Do you fear the empress so much that you would rather hide?"

The Buzzard, Sybon, said nothing. Fitz raised a brow.

"I certainly hope so."

With that, he flicked his wrist and sent Sybon the Buzzard out of sight. He never once looked back.

"Now...."

Fitz stood firm against his mauled arm, fur still madly stained of his chocolate blood. He gestured to the fountain and maybe to Zoe or Zack. Then his head turned atop his worm neck, slowly approaching his massive amber eyes for Damon. His mangled arm reached out in solitude.

"The remote, if you please."

Damon's brain hardly flinched when the words zeroed in on his understanding. He plucked Zack's ball and tossed it over to Fitz's waiting palm. Fitz turned away. He approached the fountain with a silent calm. Damon noticed at the corner of his eye, Zoe backed off, her body shivering like she'd been freshly dunked in arctic waters.

"My lord, Emperor Zachary of the Great Lord Azeroth," Fitz called.

Zack lifted his swollen face at once. "Yes?" His lungs shook as he spoke.

"Do you remember what I have taught you of this place?" Fitz gestured at the fountain and then across the trees. Damon couldn't quite see anything, but he could feel it—an energy force so fresh and clean. The fountain must have something to do with it. It'd be the only thing logical enough to keep this hilltop from being swallowed by that toxic rain of smoke and fire beyond the thorns.

Zack nodded silently. Something gnawed at his brain. Damon could tell.

Fitz nodded, "Good. Then I expect you to wait at the lip once I have activated the portal. Lord Damon?" His eyes again perched themselves on Damon. "I shall explain the matter once our emperor has passed through."

Damon nodded. He couldn't find any words to say.

"And now, for our first step."

Zoe broke out of her awkward perch. "First step?" She sent a ravenous caw right for Fitz. "Who exactly arranged this meeting anyway?"

Damon stared at Fitz. Fitz returned the stare, his amber eyes doubling their usual glow.

Up in the air, Zoe's hand flew. "Great!" she scatted. "Just absolutely…."

"Zoe!" Damon shouted. She turned his way, scowl at the helm.

"What?"

"It's too late to turn back," Damon answered, short on thought. "We can't just…." Thoughts began wondering in. His eyes met hers at an ever-changing angle. She missed something out of this conversation. He could tell that by the way she pierced his heart with those ebony marble eyes.

Then that question had to roll off his tongue. "How much do you know?"

Fitz began, "As much as I…." but Zoe beat him to the punch.

"Nothing!" she shrieked. "Listen, Mister Fish Bait! I haven't the slightest over your ideals for Zack or for Damon for that matter. Their parents should be telling us where to go next, not you."

Damon found his chance.

"They took off!" he hooked off his right cheek. "Dad took off with Mom. They left us with nothing to go on. Not a word, Zoe."

Zoe's figure began to relax. She returned to the fountain and perched there, quiet as a curious raven. Damon took her nod as the sign.

He explained, "Fitz is our guardian right now."

"You made this decision," Fitz corrected, shooing Zoe off the fountain. "It was you who chose the path—and the will—to recover your parents from their retreat

"Here you stand, victorious in your will to rescue your brother, however little we took a part of. You are properly united…."

"And we got you, too, Mister Fuzzy!" Zack boasted. "Heck, yeah! I can't wait to kick some alien butt after this."

"You're not doing anything!" Zoe shot. "As soon as the fire's out, we're going back to the car and…."

"Car's toast," Damon smiled. "I checked."

Fitz cleared his throat. "May I suggest an appropriate solution?"

"By all means," said Zoe. She didn't look pleased.

"Thank you," Fitz bowed. He rolled Zack's ball into a cup slot along the fountain's lip. Again, he waved Zoe away, shooing her like some sort of rodent. She gave him a mountainous scowl, but he never seemed to mind.

He wrapped his magnet gauntlet upon the ball and, like the door in the cavern, twisted to the right. The fountain shook off a fleck of dust, but did nothing more. Nodding at the obelisk, Fitz walked a third away around the fountain, always keeping his hand on the ball. The entire fountain mimicked him exactly, shrieking as metal on metal. Damon didn't mind this particular noise. He had heard enough explosions and alien noise in the last week. Shrieking metal bands were too ordinary for the ears now.

A clicking noise ripped through the ground. Damon trampled on the grass, minding the nothingness that crept at his ankles.

Here, Fitz tugged the ball back.

The stones dropped from their nests all at once. The bitter splash of water trickled Damon's shoes. He couldn't care less. They were beyond clean now that he had gone through pretty near a hailstorm of events to get to this spot. Seesh! He should have opted for a second set before he left the cottage.

His mind wondered for a moment. How long ago did he leave for the fountain that first time? A day? No! A week. Yeah, there was that couple of days of nothing, or so Fitz said.

Ah, who cared? The fountain split apart anyway. It was...

...It was...

"It's splitting apart!"

All eyes pounded on Damon. He stared back at these eyes, one person at a time. His mouth grew dry. He couldn't help that outburst.

Fitz raised a finger, naturally.

"Eyes away from the vortex."

"What vortex?" Damon blinked. He crept closer to the spectacle, mind ever wondering past the limits of his logic. Curiosity had always been in his favour.

All the while, Fitz had drawn himself back from the fountain, as did the others. The fountain itself had split into three. Each part dragged along the concrete slabs, again like metal on metal. The water spilt out what remained of the bowl, the obelisk receding into whatever the fountain had been hiding all this time.

Damon still felt the tug of curiosity drag him closer. Not even Fitz's shouts could snip this cord from Damon's bindings. Slowly, he made it to the edge, and then his head drew over....

Over the edge and into a blistering fire of whites and blue.

He drew back before the blue could get to him. Too late with the white, though. It was going to take a bit for those burn blots to ebb away. Blinking didn't help, nor did rubbing and all this shouting on either side of him.

"Do not throw a blind ear so deliberately."

Deaf ear, Damon thought. *Deaf ear, Fitz.*

"You crazy, dude!" Zack boasted. "That's what I like. Me like it *goooood*!"

"Shut up, twit!"

That was Zoe, speaking out of character once more. What did the Hive ship do to her personality?

"Easy everyone," Fitz said somewhere in this fuzzy mess. "Let us catch our bearings and observe the moment. The portal still requires a moment before it can tear itself open. I understand it has not been used for a considerable amount of...."

"What about the stones?" Zack shouted.

"The ball stays," Fitz answered. "It cannot be undone from its prison."

"Not the metal ball, Mister Fuzzy!" Zack squirmed. "The Elder stones!"

"Oh..." Fitz grew quiet. Damon still couldn't find anyone in this fuzz. He lurched ahead, toward the distant trees. He thought he saw Dad's arm for a moment.

"Oh!" Fitz said, alarmed. "Hurry! Gather them before they fall in!"

Feet trampled the earth. Stone clattered against stone. People fussed. A worm dog sighed. A portal hummed. Yup, all while Damon was stuck in the middle of flat earth, trying to make sense of his sight. What could have possibly come next? Zack hollering a crude remark at him?

"Hey!" said the younger brother. "How about hauling your big fat...?"

"Zack!"

Yup, Damon nodded, precisely that. He led himself out of the framework and onto dry land. Maybe a little breather would do.

The blots were good as gone. Damon blinked. Yeah, he could get back to this commotion.

Or he could say his last goodbyes.

"Oh my God!"

"Zoe!"

"Sorry."

She couldn't help it. Damon couldn't blame her. She probably hadn't seen a dead body before, and neither had he, not in the state Dad was in.

It seemed too messy to touch, too messy to look at. Damon couldn't take a single blink before turning back. All that time watching gory movies and forensic dramas couldn't save his grace. His stomach couldn't handle the load.

"Okay," Zack sighed. "Who let the dead body in here?"

Damon spun for his brother, fists pumping for action. "That dead body is our Dad, punk!"

Zack scowled, his face reminding Damon how bad grapefruit shriveled his tongue. "But you guys said..."

"Not in front of him!" Fitz exclaimed warningly. "Do not speak your father's troubles before the remains of his host."

Damon zoned out for a moment. He homed in on the dents on his bat. They didn't look so big—a few here and there, mostly from batting those magnetic rings around.

He remembering how Dad used to teach him how to aim and strike at a pitch. He remembered he rarely missed the ball during his feats at the minors, no matter how hard the pitchers hooked it. And even if someone did catch it or tags him out later on, all his classmates—all his friends—cheered him on. To them, he was still the baseball champion.

He aimed to use this bat for all the wrong reasons. Even in his deranged state, Grandpa always told him: "Never swing because you're angry. People get killed that way."

If only Grandpa knew what life had in store for them.

"My lord!"

Fitz's words finally broke through Damon's mental block.

"Yeah?" Damon stuttered. "Sorry. Got carried away...." His words broke before he could finish.

"The portal is ready," Fitz announced. "You may observe and lead us to our destination at your own discretion."

Damon took his time to the lip, eyes weary of Fitz's presence. "As much as I want to lead, Fitz, I don't think it'd be a good.... Woah!"

Peeking over, his words stopped shy of the ledge. They could not pass the dizziness pricking his brain. First came the pinning vortex of shimmering light. A space of blank or some sort of white took the middle, either swirling or swiping Damon's eyes with a total lack of shape and colour. It felt like his eyelids peeled over like some sort of negative censor on those blooper shows.

A few blinks and the so-called sensor faded away. In its place, a more convenient setting brushed upon his heart. He felt welcomed by the portal's awkward hum and its presentation of an otherwise dim room.

But then, something felt wrong with the picture, something Damon couldn't quite catch at the peak of the moment. He....

Wait a second!

His eyes were met with a sudden lack of logic. Staring right at him was a room filled with metallic arches and a floor that could very well be old grey rock. The floor itself wasn't way at the back. No, there're two cylinder doors there, each complimenting the other.

No, the door was past Damon's feet, on his side of the portal. The room defied gravity in every way.

Suddenly, leaping out of the frying pan didn't feel like a good idea any more.

Leaping off the Frying Pan

"Confusing, isn't it?"

"Eh?"

"Confusing," Fitz said. "Yes, I had that feeling myself, several times."

Damon broke out of a stare. "What? You're reading my mind again?" he scowled.

Fitz shook his head with a girly wave. "Oh, no, just assuming." His answer didn't peel a flake of truth in Damon's ears.

"BONZAI!"

All eyes jerked toward the source of Zack's charging cry. Damon meant to shoot back the stop sign, but the little brat already leapt his way in. Damon's curiosity took over, eying the slump that was Zack.

The brat made it through the portal without touching any of the edges. He tried one of his famous cannonballs, maybe because the portal looked like water at the most acute angles. Through and through Zack went. Not once did the portal refract, pulse, or did anything that would suggest that something had gone through it. Damon awed a breath; he was impressed.

Then gravity took over and slammed Zack into the floor. Swirls of dust encompassed the brat, exposing a grate-patterned metal tile beneath. Maybe the whole floor was like that. One thing for sure, no one had used the other side of this portal for a good long while.

Zack mumbled something under his breath. His body staggered like a lump of deformed mushrooms for maybe a step or two.

Damon couldn't hold the laughter back. "Zack, are you okay?"

"Whatever," Zack answered coldly. "Now I know how you feel.... Argh!"

Damon turned to Fitz with a raised brow. "Could you read his thoughts for a...?"

Fitz quickly shook his head. "As much as there is a temporal displacement before our feet, my mind cannot penetrate it. As you would say, he is out of range."

Damon cocked an eyebrow. "You sure? I mean, who's the furthest you can read?"

Fitz pointed to Zoe. "The fundamentals of this portal disrupt the accessibility of whoever may roam your cottage during the disruption."

"Meaning?"

"I can read no more than two minds, who are neither in the condition to think." Fitz turned toward the south. "I do believe they will reach the river's edge...Oh! And one vanished from my sight completely."

Knots tugged in Damon's gut. "Dead?"

Fitz shook his head. "Not in the slightest. They are out of range. The other, I fear, is caught.... No, his demise is imminent."

"Okay," Zoe shot in. "I think I heard enough of that. Is it safe for me to jump in now?" She stepped up to the plate, eyes on the portal, and then on Fitz. "I mean, I won't get cancer like I would if I was to eat at McDonald's?"

"Absolutely," Fitz nodded. "I would prefer, however, that Lord Damon be the proper lead in this case."

"Ladies first," Damon sighed. "I still can't figure out..."

"Out of my way then!" Zoe pushed. She gave a shot hop and a leapt at the ledge then leaned forward. Her body sprung out at the last moment, and as though it were natural, she walked through the portal and onto the metal floor like it was nothing.

Again, Damon held his head back. How could she do that so well?

Crap! That sick feeling in his stomach was really getting to him. He needed something to break away from it, something simple, like a question. Oh, that was it.

"Uh, Fitz?"

The worm dog lifted his eyes from the shimmer of the portal. Somehow, the blue and white didn't refract off his orbs so gently.

"Yes, my lord?"

Damon hesitated. "I'm only wondering," he said. "What about the stones? Didn't you say they're sensitive to this sort of thing?"

"In a way," Fitz sighed, holding one of the stones to his breastplates. "I didn't notice any fluctuation in the vortex when Zoe or the emperor leapt through."

Damon opened his mouth, but Zack beat his words to the starting line. "Stop calling me that!" exclaimed the brute. "I'm just Zack."

"Your title has already been appointed to you the day you were conceived," said Fitz, his eyes wandering toward Damon. "Trust me, I know."

Damon returned a stoned stare. Uh, that didn't sound right.

"Whatever?" cried Zoe. "Get your butt in here, okay?"

"Oh, sure," Damon shook. "Right. I'm on my way."

"Stop yapping' and jump in already!" Again, this was Zoe. Seesh! What an attitude.

Damon took one quick glance of faith. His eyes intercepted Fitz, but Fitz did not look back. The worm dog seemed distanced on something. Maybe those shimmering things in the portal's vortex had a different effects on his kind.

He turned away from Fitz, finally realizing his own misstep. A quick push and a false drop pushed him through what felt like a torrential downpour in the middle of the Amazon. Then his whole head spun like gravity pulled a prank. He hit the ground, rump first, and then head. The impact, rather, bounce, of the metal drove a white-knuckled fuzz in his nose.

Zack poured out the laughter. "Owned!" he cried, dancing like it was some disco party. Damon forgot the year.

"Okay, Zack," Damon stressed. "I get your point." How he managed to push those words out his mouth was beyond him. He could barely roll onto his knees as it was. This gravity shift really messed with his brain.

A massive sneeze blew half his sinuses through his nose. It had better not be from all the dust drifting around the floor.

"Mind the dust," a voice called from behind, distorted by the portal's generous hum. Damon turned around, limping with each shuffle. The portal stood right there, hardly two feet ahead. He quickly shuffled back, noting how the outer rings embedded themselves into the floor. This all-too-familiar design reminded Damon of his trip through Toronto's subway a few years back. Wasn't it a class trip to the Royal Ontario Museum or something?

Beyond the shimmer and the emptiness was a sky marked with smoke and despair, yet it seemed to be distorted by some awkward fairy dust or energy field, definitely not from the portal, though. It was a different shade of blue altogether.

"Fancy landing, my lord."

Damon rubbed the back of his head. "Don't mention it."

"Okay, then," Zoe said, half-stretching like a yoga star. "What's to do next?"

"Through one of those doors," Damon answered, a short nod taking him. "I want to see where we are."

"Good enough, then. How about we.... Look out!"

Zoe's wild stare came too late. Damon hardly flinched an inch when all ready, a load of weights crashed into his back. He toppled to the floor, arm and forehead first. The dust splattered in his nose. A sneezing fit ensured.

He tried standing himself again, but it was no use. The weight pinned him like a bag of excess clothes. It stank of wet dog.

"Fitz!" someone cried.

"Don't move!" another answered.

Neither voice could connect with Damon's ears. His brain rattled so much that Zoe really did sound like Zack. The portal hum might have something to do with it.

A third voice called from afar. This one Damon could differentiate from the others. It belonged to Sybon, no doubt about it. Too bad Damon couldn't shift out of this mess. Too bad his eyes were layered with that annoying blur.

"Ha!" said the Buzzard. "So carried away you've become. Where's that guard of yours, filth? Should you have not been paying attention to my thoughts? Or did you think I was the one caught in the flames?"

"Fitz, get up!"

"It's no use, Zachary. He's out cold. Damon, too."

"Call me Zack!"

And call me dumb, Damon thought. He could still hear. He could still see, if just a little. And yet he couldn't move with this big lump of Fitz pinning him down. All that armour plating and chain mail—it'd be no wonder Fitz couldn't stand half the time.

"Oh ho!" said Sybon. "Bickering amongst yourselves all ready? Here! I have a little toy for you to play with!"

"Shut up!" That must've been Zack. He always did bicker when someone treated him like a five-year old.

"Such a primitive language you speak," said Sybon. "May I suggest a thermo nuclear detonator to plug that mouthpiece of yours?"

"Oh, God!"

That was Zoe, of course. Zack, no matter how foul his mind was, could never speak that name in vain. With Dad and Fitz training him half his life, Damon could see why.

"What's that?" Zack piped, probably referring to this so-called detonator.

"What do you think, you inferior brat?"

Sybon sounded only a little more like Mom when Zack kept slamming the screen door that one night. Zack must've broken the Buzzard's nerves, too.

A node of silence plugged Damon's ears. It was like one of those games where a bomb would go off near the player and the sound effects go mute, but the music kept playing. Only here, rather than music, Damon heard the faintest of the portal hum like it'd been moved back a few dozen meters.

No, it was further. It was like someone pulled the portal away. Yet, he couldn't help but notice the dust flickering in his face. He'd sneeze if it wasn't for Fitz slumping over him. Something seemed to be sprawling closer, and yet, the blur wouldn't go away. If only he could rub from his eyes.

Then the ground left him completely. Darkness swallowed him, only to be replaced by a sickening yellow light. He could hear voices somewhere in front of the portal's generous hum, but even they were blurred out. It was like his whole body blurred out of his senses.

It must be the dust. It could be alien dust, the kind with those alien germs that humans grow severe allergic reactions to. Yeah, that'd explain all the sudden fuzziness.

The amber receded, so did the dust and the blur. Suddenly, his whole body stiffened to the frigid floor like he'd been slapped on a glacier in Midwestern Alberta. Damon wondered for a moment. What if he got to see something more spectacular on Dad hunting adventure?

The ground shook, but Damon hardly heard a noise. Here, he noticed a dip or a bowl on the floor. No, that was the shape of this room. It was a hollow sphere, completely reddish in tint, could be rust. Damon doubted it.

Finally, he felt the strength to pull himself out of the tangle of worm dog and flashy limbs. His mindset couldn't place direction yet. He probably had to scan the dim room about three times before he could finally see a neon yellow square. A silhouette peeked from beneath the rectangle, obstructing its well-curved presence.

What was that? Someone's head?

Damon tried to muster. He tried calling someone's name, but his mind couldn't decide who.

First, he tried Zack, but no sound came out. Then he tried Zoe, and then Fitz. Nothing. The air was as dead as desert soil.

He staggered to one knee. It bit him with a bone splintering pain. A short shove with his hands allowed him to push up. His knee still hated him. He pushed a little harder.

A little more....

There! His good knee was in place. Now he needed some solid support, something other than Fitz, another push or maybe a wobble. The ascent, slow and feeble, grew throughout the far reaches of his fingers and toes. The energy sapped from him by Fitz's tumble started to pour back into him. He felt alive again.

Then, darkness came—complete pitch black. Damon couldn't see the bridge of his nose or the droop of his eyebrows. His hands stumbled onto fur, then onto solid metal. The metal felt stingy, almost scorched. He could barely touch it without chirping a little whelp of pain. He heard someone call back to him.

"Damon? Is that you?"

"Right here, Zack."

"Good." There was a deep breath of sorts. Then came a cluster of words Damon could barely sort out. "Man-that-was-weird-did-you-see-that?"

"Hunh?" Damon didn't stare. He didn't know which direction to look.

"That weird blue lady?" Zack said. "Didn't you...Ah, forget it."

Damon shrugged. That was fine by him.

"Where's the lights?" he said.

"Don't ask me," Zack piped. "Try looking for a button on the wall."

"Uh, thanks..." Ow! The metal stung, real bad. "Thanks, Zack, but I don't think I can touch anything.... But Fitz, of course." Metal then fur again. Damon was going around in circles. That wet dog stink had better go away soon. He could feel a sneezing fit tickling his horizon.

The Other Nervous Wreck

How long it took to get lighting in this wretched hole, Damon couldn't care less. At least it was over. At least he found his light switch outside the lip of the one open door.

Too bad his sneezing fit hit him like an anvil to the nose. Dust fluttered and swirled everywhere, reminding Damon of those snowstorms, the one where it snowed endless feathers rather than ice particles. Where did it come from?

The amber light from the hollow sphere didn't last long beyond the open door. It didn't help solve the matter in the portal room, either. Scorch marks littered the window on the other side.

"Oh, that's why the wall's so freaking hot!" Zack exclaimed. "I didn't think the big boom could do that." Big boom always meant an explosion.

"What explosion?" said Damon, only to get that stare Zack inherited from Mom. "Stop staring like that!" Damon snapped back. Zack snorted out of one enlarged nostril and looked the other way. At least Damon didn't have to throw a fist this time.

"What explosion?" he asked again.

"You sound like a stupid parrot!" Zack spat.

Damon pushed the limit breaker. "What explosion, Zack?"

Silence.

Utter silence. Damon's limit breaker worked like a charm.

It took a brief walk around the room, but Zack managed to force an answer out of himself somehow. "Fine!" he stomped, his foot landing shy of Fitz's fuzzy tail. "The portal blew up, okay? Zi-borg threw in some tennis ball in the shimmering stuff."

"Thermo nuclear detonator."

Zack's face sprung to life. Fitz's body shuffled. The worm dog was awake.

"Mister Fuzzy!" Zack exclaimed. Fitz seemed to take no note of the brat's excitement.

"Haven't I told you?" lipped the worm dog. "Buzzards carry thermonuclear detonators as part of their standard equipment."

Damon paid little attention to the details. He couldn't help but notice the lack of limp in Fitz's feeble leg as the worm dog straddled to his feet.

Fitz scratched the back of his neck, muttering something under breath.

"What was that?" Damon asked impulsively. He thought he heard a curse in there.

"No, no," Fitz replied. "Normally, such a device would have little impact on the surrounding area. It is usually meant to sting a group of targets within a specified area. But throwing one in the disruption field?" He turned to Zack. "Are you certain he had done so?"

Zack nodded excitedly. Fitz turned back to Damon, his face hung in a lowly scowl.

"Such an action would cause the disruption field to balloon chaotically. Everything would be sucked into a vortex of tremendous strength."

"Like a black hole?" Damon pondered aloud.

"Yes," Fitz answered slowly. "But in a very different manner."

Then came the weirdest silence of all. Fitz stood in the center of the room staring at nothing. Zack seemed too spaced out with his own sense of glee. Damon couldn't be bothered snapping his brother out of it. He tried the snapping finger in Fitz's face instead.

"Fitz!" he called, remembering the incident with the Buzzard in the ship's windshield. Again, there came no response. That bizarre tint of violet trickled around the edges of the pupils affixed in Fitz's great owl eyes.

"Hey!" Zack suddenly barked. He stomped his foot again, this time planting the heel of his boot directly into the bridge of Fitz's tail. The worm dog yelped like a dog freshly whipped by a rolled-up newspaper. The stark break in the air caused Damon to topple back and out of the sphere.

His hand caught the ledge of the light switch on the way out. The door slammed shut, missing the tips of his fingers by a scratch of an inch.

The lack of support clung to Damon's arms. He scrambled for something to fall onto other than all this dust that kept attacking his sinuses.

Failure.

His landing ended with a furious fit of sneezing, one burst right after another. By the time that was over, Damon had to find a good pocket of fresh air to tackle. There was something about it, something grimy that made his lungs want to gasp for more air.

Then again, if there was so much dust on the floor and this was nowhere near home, then the air in this place was probably stale—stale and full of oxygen. Despite all this hacking and sneezing, not once did Damon feel out of shape. In fact, his arms and legs felt like they defied the last couple of years of sports and other types of stress. He wondered if Grandpa would have gotten some good out of it. Who knew? He'd might have even put some life in this dead place.

Thump-thump!

Damon blinked. A bitter form of shadow broke the amber glistening in his eyes. A short glance up and the door's minute rectangular window caught his attention.

Zack stood directly behind, pounding and mouthing words that couldn't quite reach Damon's ears. The lack of light in this next room dropped too much shadow on the brat's mouth.

"Stop talking!" Damon snapped back. His words came upon a deaf door rattling of pounding fists, so it seemed.

Up on his feet he went, blistering red at the cheeks. He pushed right at the door—his fingers felt like melting—and stared Zack straight in the eyes. That seemed to work. The brat suddenly stopped yapping. The door stopped rattling, and soon, Fitz took the picture frame. Damon nodded. He shut his eyes and pretended there was no door at all.

"Quite a predicament you put on us," said Fitz. His voice was right next to Damon's ears, and yet, Damon could feel no breath brushing against his lobes. He ignored the lack of presence and focused on image. Fitz spoke in his thoughts.

"Sorry," Damon sighed. "I didn't see..."

"Speak up. Your voice is hard to reach through this metal."

Damon cleared his throat. "I'm sorry," he said a little louder. "What's going on? Why's Zack freaking out?"

"The other door is jammed," said Fitz. "It looks like it has fused somewhat on the other side. I suspect what our emperor have witnessed may have something to do with it."

"Figures," said Damon.

"Excuse me?"

"The explosion!" Damon barked. "Zack mentioned the explosion, Fitz. You said something..."

Fitz raised a finger of note. "A moment, please."

A gleam of gold struck Damon on the eyelids. He opened them to find the window empty. A quick shot in revealed Zack and Fitz gabbing over something. Their lips buzzed too fast for Damon to understand.

Fitz paced back to the window, eyes shut and stubby arms crossed behind his shoulders. Damon quickly shut his eyes, drawing a sharp breath to the lungs. A tickle of dust spat out a cough, but Damon could handle it. The air didn't feel so bad now that Fitz thought about something.

"Okay," said Fitz. "It appears we may come upon a situation. I will require our emperor's assistance..."

"Call him Zack!" Damon shot mid thought.

"Do not interrupt!" Fitz snapped. "I require our emperor's assistance. We must force the other hatch a slight of your foot more. Our emperor..."

Fitz's voice spat a sudden moment of silence. Damon pictured Zack mouthing off about this emperor crap. Not that it mattered, the brat being muted like this felt kind of fun.

"Excuse me," Fitz said. "Zachary..." Another lapse of silence. "Zack will crawl through the space and observe the matter."

"How about Zoe?" Damon spat suddenly. Oh, crap! How could he forget about her? She wasn't even in the sphere with them when the portal exploded.

"She appears safe for the time being," Fitz answered. Damon felt insecure with the wording. He was avoiding something.

"Uh..."

Damon snapped from his mental room. Owl eyes still beamed at him from behind the window.

"Yes, Fitz?"

"We will be unable to use this door," said the worm dog. "The mechanism for this particular sealing hatch is damaged well beyond repair. I will require a task of you."

Damon smirked. "Run around to the other door and open it. Yup. Gotcha loud and clear, Fitz." He finished with a snappy salute.

Fitz's eyelids rolled on sharp angles. "You do not sound impressed."

"Uh, that's because I'm new here, Fitz," Damon answered, his tone as sharp as Fitz's eyelids. "How about mentioning that the other door's damaged beyond repair, too, eh?"

"Foolish," Fitz giggled. "I already made my observation on such a point. You merely require passing through the first passage on the right. Take another right, and you shall reach the open hatch in quick time."

Damon turned to the nothingness behind him. "Don't have a flashlight, either," he noted. "You wouldn't suppose...?"

"Do not be concerned of the lighting," Fitz interrupted. "Your eyes should be capable of adjusting once you've reached the limit of this lighting."

"Fitz," Damon growled, "you're asking the impossible again."

"Am I now?"

Fitz stepped away from the window. In a short blink, the amber light sparked off. Damon thought he could hear Zack screaming. Then again, that could've been from the black all the way behind him.... Or in front of him.

Aw, crap! Now he had done it.

He was lost as a needle in a haystack of pitch dark. When he found yet another wall between him and Zack, the lights went out and he had to start drawing the whole picture from start *yet again*.

Nice one, Fitz....

Wait a sec. What was that light way in the back there?

Damon wondered out of his safe zone. His feet shuffled against the gritty floor, somewhere a mixture between rock and rusted metal. The dust didn't pick up so harsh here. There might have been more recent traffic in this blackness.

The light fuzzed neatly across the wall like a beam of light drawing itself behind...Plastic? Or was it glass? No, it was too glossy and yet so tough looking. Damon reached for it, but it was still too far for his arms. Hmm.... Maybe this room wasn't so small after all.

The light streaked on. It streaked on in a distance well beyond Damon's measure. He trained his eyes on its direction. This must be what Fitz meant.

He made do with a rust spot here and there, always following this bizarre streak of neon blue. Its radiance grew with every beat Damon's heart tapped. But rather than metal structures, Damon could only get glimpse of a barren wall of pale grey rock. He noted brief glitters upon the ledges of these rough cuts, but he couldn't decide if it was the dust or the elements bound inside the stone.

Damon bit his lip. Zack first, curiosity later. He trekked on, doubling his pace. A break in the light signaled his move to break right. A fierce amber glow streamed through the floor of a new tunnel that was all metal. This was better, but not by far. The crystal amber feeling on the hive-like walls seemed to blur the line between dreams and reality. Damon felt like he'd been here before, and yet, he could never remember ever walking down a corridor full of hive-like designs.

Hmph. Must be the dust again.

Oh, a door! Damon dared himself to stop. He failed. Zack kept pressing his mind, his panic trigger. Damon couldn't help but fret. Why did he always find himself in the wrong situation whenever he was in a new place? Why couldn't he sit down, walk around, and feed his curiosity instead?

No! A family needed him. Zack needed him to open that other door. There was no other way to get back to him, not under their current status, and from what Fitz has been hinting, not even he knew their situation well enough.

On his feet he went, triple the speed. This tunnel had to stop somewhere. It had better not be one of those dead end doors that never opened. This wasn't one of those video games, not at all.

Damon counted three doors on his right and two on his left. He never took the extra time to guess the distances between one another. They could have been spaced out evenly, but the way this tunnel arched away from where he needed, there must be something rather decent between one of his right doors and the portal room.

The tunnel finally broke free. Damon found himself in yet another large space. The lighting in here felt more pleasant. Damon could see the walls and the floor, probably because he counted three of those streaking blue lights this time. Odd, though. He couldn't quite catch sight of the ceiling. The aurora of the light didn't want to reach for some reason. Maybe the rock walls weren't reflective enough.

Weird. Very weird.

Then Fitz's voice rolled out of the dark, completely out of nowhere.

"I sense your thoughts so soon?"

Damon clutched his ears, his feet suddenly still. His heart pounded against a flapping chest. This telepathy felt so freakish, and yet, it was the only way either of them could talk to each other. If only Damon had something that made it feel like something else. How about a walkie-talkie headset like those SWAT teams on TV have?

"Damon, could you pay attention?" Fitz said wearingly. "We have a situation that requires your upmost intervention, and you simply cannot control your focus."

Damon broke from his stare. "Sorry." He broke into his double pace, speeding against the grain of the blazing blue streaks. "Sorry, Fitz. I think I need a breather soon."

"And you shall receive one," Fitz answered, "but only once we have established our current situation. I am counting on you as you are aware."

"All right, Fitz!" Damon roared. Seesh! That worm dog's a mouthful to handle. How *do you turn this telepathy link off?*

"I heard that," clipped Fitz.

"Shut up!" Damon bounced back. His brain felt like gelatin for the moment.

Amber light spilled in Damon's eyes. A glisten of blue surrounded it in an unearthly fashion. Damon stopped a moment and winced his eyes. The neon blue bent itself around the hatch in nearly a perfect circle. It hovered around the base of the stone walls a little odd, but at least it looked cool.

Damon stormed the hatch. No sooner did he reach it than his hands found the switch for this side. He tapped it on his way in, his legs building up some speed. One door slammed behind him, the other sinking effortlessly into its groove. The wind changed focus here, shifting from a cool earthly grey to a boiling metallic red. Damon's nostrils shriveled with a kind of scorch he recognized from the burning forest back home.

Eerie.

The scorch alone should have said it all, but Damon's eyes had to be sure. From the open hatch, he could tell they were cut off from Grandpa's lot. Only a partial sphere of crisped molten metal remained of the portal itself. There were no rings, no platform lip to walk off—nothing.

He hardly took one step into the portal room when Zack's voice attacked him on all fronts.

"Glad you made it."

"Shut it!"

Zack grew a sobbing scowl. "I wasn't sarcastic, you jerk!"

Damon pointed the finger. "Blame Fitz. For some dumb reason, he won't stop reading my head."

"That dumb reason," Fitz began. He tapered off before Damon could hear the rest. Damon couldn't be bothered to ask for a repeat.

His eyes shifted to where Fitz rested on his knees. Zoe sprawled across the ground in front of him, clothes mildly scorched. Another partial sphere rested here in the floor, but its surface looked much rougher, like it was carved out with an ice cream spoon over and over. The edges of this crater, however, were melted all the same as the larger crater.

Damon stared at either. He couldn't make which end was the talkative one.

"What's going on here?" he said impulsively. His brain didn't have the nerve to think the puzzle through.

"The blue lady saved us," Zack piped up. "It was so cool, Damon. You really should've seen it."

Damon shot a glare to Fitz's way. The worm dog repulsed with a toothy scowl.

"What?"

"Remember when I mentioned the Illori?"

Damon's brain fizzled. Fitz shook his head, a growling sigh brushing from his lips.

"The Illori!" snapped the worm dog. "My lord, Zack. Do you remember what I have taught you?"

Zack stared. Damon stepped in.

"Forget it, Fitz," he said. "Zack wouldn't last five seconds at school without..."

"Shut up!" Zack exploded. "Yeah, you did say something, Mister Fuzzy. They were evil wizards who eat people's hearts."

"Souls," Fitz grunted.

"Same difference!" Zack scowled. He turned that scowl on Damon. "Yeah, I paid attention, Damon. So why don't you shut up and let...?"

Damon took Zack by the collar, but Fitz had already pushed him back. "Now is not the time for a family feud," he warned. "We have a delicate situation up front, and we have many arising situations in the near future. Until we are at least capable of knowing our most direct route, I shall bar you from striking your brother."

"Ha ha!" Zack stuck. Fitz turned his evil owl stare his way.

"That goes for you, too."

Zack's tongue went limp. He shut his mouth before Fitz could manage his scruffy throat again.

Damon turned his eye to Zoe. Fitz knelt beside her. His hands never went near her, yet his magnet gauntlet illuminated with a mean red through its fine print.

"What are you doing?" Damon clipped impulsively.

"Sealing the demon inside her," sighed the worm dog. "Alas, had it not been for the Illorul's swift thinking, there would be nothing left of this room." His head lifted, eyes trained on Damon. "Nor would we."

Damon crimpled his face. "And yet you're shutting...did you say demon?"

"Now is not the time to..."

Damon didn't bother to let Fitz finish. He scooped the worm dog off his front knees with a stern grip on the upper shoulders. A harsh shove and Damon found the room he needed to clamp Fitz's wounded shoulder with his foot. Fitz winced, but his face showed little of the pressure Damon applied.

"Talk!"

Fitz rested perfectly still. His tail did not lash. His hands and feet did not scratch. He laid motionless on the floor, save for his heaving chest and his wild frantic stare.

"Talk!" Damon demanded.

"It is rather difficult to describe," Fitz said, twiddling his stubby thumbs. "Could you...Ack! At least remove your foot from my shoulder. I shall explain what is necessary."

Damon slipped his foot from the armpit. He staggered back, mindful of the partial sphere and Zoe's outstretched hand. Faint jogs of his memory rushed back over the past few days. He was sure Fitz has mentioned the Illori before but never in a concrete manner. This Damon knew because he would have known what these so-called Illori truly were.

"The Illori," said Fitz, "are of a silicon-based realm far beyond the reaches of this universe. I should know, I have felt one's presence within me once...twice, perhaps. Their souls are much easier to read than the hybrids of your nature.

"In a sense, the Illori are not meant to roam this universe. We carry no predator or disease that would dispatch of them in a natural manner. And to be honest, every last one of us in this Known Galaxy are as easy game to them as the last."

"Hunh?" Zack blasted. "Game? Like in black people?"

"No!" Damon burst, slapping the brat across the back of his head. "Zack, he means food, like the deer Grandpa used to hunt back...." He hesitated for a moment.

"Where home used to be, the Illori eat us.

"They consume our souls, to be honest," Fitz pointed. "As I've mentioned earlier to both of you, the Illori require a certain amount of spiritual energy in order to cast their powers upon their intended prey. In their realm, they would feast on two—maybe three—souls of high intelligence to last them for the least duration of three weeks.

"However, those who were trapped in our realm grew weaker with each passing Terran day. Their energy depletes in manner best described as an allergy, as your father was once allergic to peanuts."

Damon smirked. "You know there's a neat little fix for that. Feed the victim little bits of their allergy at a time. Their body gets used to it after a while. Grandpa did that with me once. Got the tomatoes to actually stop filling my mouth with cankers."

Fitz shook his head. "It is never that simple with the Illori, I fear. They.... *Omph!*"

Fitz made it to both hind feet but slumped forward, his wounded arm catching the ground first. A blistering bark snapped through the air.

"You hurt him!" Zack growled. "You hurt Mister..."

"I didn't hurt him," Damon answered. "Dad did." A boot landed square on his shins. He played hopscotch long enough to force the driving pain out his ears.

"Liar!" Zack bellowed. "You hurt Mister Fuzzy, didn't you?"

"Lord Damon is correct," Fitz grunted. "He never initialized any harm upon me. Your father, Zack, has become rogue."

Zack spat a wad at Fitz's feet. "I trusted you!"

Damon caught his forearm and tugged down. "You listen to me, you little punk!" he registered. "Don't you even think of spitting again, or I'll give you a bloody nose, you understand?"

"Let go!" Zack screamed. Damon squeezed harder.

"Do I make myself clear, Zack?"

"You're not my father!"

"Oh, yeah?" said Damon, "Well I'm still your older brother. And guess what? Dad's not here to boss me around, either. So that puts me in charge of you."

"On the contrary..." Fitz began. Damon cut him off.

"I'm not in the mood for that," he pointed. "Zack, whatever spit you have left, you swallow it, and then you help me listen, all right?"

"You're still not my father!" Zack wailed. "Let me go or I'll spit on you, too!"

Damon loosened his grip. He tried a different approach, a calmer voice like Zoe did sometimes. "What's wrong with Fitz?"

Zack's eyes spilled tears upon salt red cheeks. "Mister Fuzzy said...He said that Dad would never do that unless he broke something important. Dad's too nice to break anything, isn't he, Damon?"

"Your father disrupted an oath he swore in blood," Fitz answered wearingly. "He meant to keep the stones for himself and leave Damon with no knowledge of my presence within the family. Is that not correct, my lord?"

Damon shook his head. "Please don't make me answer that." His stomach reeled with the utmost pain and regret of family loss. Two men died for these stones, not one of them innocent in their part.

Zack looked him in the eye. "Tell him he's a liar, Damon. Tell him, hunh?"

"He's not lying, Zack."

"Hunh?"

Damon returned the stance. "Fitz isn't lying about anything but his own plans. I watched Dad and him fight. Tried to pull them away with one of the stones. I didn't realize what it would do to Dad."

"Separate soul from host," Fitz nodded. "That is exactly how the stone meant to work. But in your father's favour, it separated his weaker body from the body who housed the stone one fateful night."

A great pause filled the room. Damon and Zack exchanged glances with each other. Fitz honed in on Zoe, her body still an eyesore for the setting. Damon thought he could see her chest heave, but everything else in the room seemed to be moving at the same time.

No, she couldn't be dead.

Fitz's voice seized the outer curves of his brain. "I assure you, she is not."

Damon pried his mouth wide open, ready to assault Fitz like Mom on Zack. But with Zack right beside him, jittering and full of the unknown torture the Buzzards put him through, Damon couldn't utter a single sound.

"Now what?"

Damon twisted his head to Zack. "Hunh?"

"Don't *hunh* me!" Zack spat. "I said, 'Now what?' So now what, Damon? What do we do to get home?"

"First, we rest," said Damon. Not a single thought deterred him. "We find out where we are, what we're supposed to do, make up a few backups on the way, and then hit the road."

"How?" Zack bellowed. "The portal blew up, stupid!"

Damon stared. "Uh, have you heard of spaceships?" Zack rolled his eyes. Fitz, on the other hand, looked spiffier on the subject.

"A fair observation, my lord. But how could you have come to such a conclusion?"

"Those caves behind that wall?" Damon threw a thumb over his shoulders. "The floor has some sort of groove in it, like a subway. I'm thinking this portal brought a few supplies from way on the other side of the galaxy like earth."

"This is Luna," Fitz interrupted. "This is Terra Tetra's single moon."

Zack stared. He let out a belch of a "Hunh?" Damon shook his head.

"Let me guess," he grunted. "This place has a cloaking device, too."

"Again, good observation, my lord," said Fitz. "However, it would be difficult to identify exactly which of the four mining facilities we currently occupy. Let us hope it is not of the older bio-electric designs."

"Hey!"

Damon's head ached. His eyes shot down to Zoe who'd shifted out of her spread eagle sleep. She rolled herself on her knees and held her chin up with her elbows. "Did I hear an explosion?" she said.

Zack blurted the obvious. "Zoe! You're up!"

"Good," Fitz nodded. "Rather than discuss matters further, let us locate the primary generator. I doubt we may tolerate this stale air for much longer than half of your terran days."

Damon doubled that. He could use something to get this annoying tickle out of his nose.

Late Warning

The frying pan grew cold. The flames have died on the stove. Even the kitchen sink stopped spitting the baseball bat out of the drain.

After a good long day of worries and complaints, Damon found himself in a room neither cold nor hot. His stomach, having taken a bit of blubbery meat and chilled fruit cocktail, could have tried for something better. Perhaps one of Mom's perfectly grilled steak or a full platter of fettuccine alfredo custom tailored by Dad's superb cooking skills would do.

Zack didn't help any.

Actually, he couldn't help. Fitz kept pulling him away like a puppet dragged off the stage. First came the generator or some big room with an enormous three-pronged claw in the middle. Simply the sight of those pipes in the ceiling drew poison to Damon's soul. He pulled Zack away from Fitz for the moment, noting the dire fear inked on the brat's pale face.

Well, at least they did get the generator started. At least they could walk past all this gloom in the transport caves. There was no life down here.

Here in this great building—Damon figured it to be about the size of downtown Trent Mills—the lighting in the walls hummed a fantastic grooves. Once in a while, the corridors would open up to a fantastic display of a terrain so alien and so bare that Damon wondered if the Sahara reached out as far as this desolate, miserable looking place.

Yet with the current placement of the moon directly facing the brilliant spectacle of Earth, the exterior lighting of the structure could only reach so far.

Fitz, of course, laid down protocol and rules the instant they reached the first workable elevator down the caverns.

"No excessive lighting outside," he commanded. "The slightest of such will breach the cloak wall. Those watching from below will grow suspicious. The man you call Bush will most certainly become involved."

Damon waved it off. It was not like the good president was going to call a nuclear strike right off the bat.

"Next," said Fitz, "we must recognize all major routes between the temporal disruption generators and the primary command tower. Also, be on the watch for any signs that would lead us to the docking bays. I am certain there are several ships available to us for short distance travel. However, the whereabouts of their former occupants would be yet known."

Zack absorbed this too well. That night, Damon found himself standing in front of a screaming brat, trying to make him forget some nightmare about spiders and white frogs invading his palace.

"There's no such thing as a white frog," Damon smirked. This led to more hassle. The evil stare he got back alone proved his answer to be wrong. Of course, there were white frogs, but they lived somewhere in South America.

Try telling that to a kid who'd believe anything. Then blame the worm dog who force-fed him a survival guide of the yonder beyond the moon.

In all of this, Zoe didn't exist. Every once in a while, Damon would see her amongst the short crowd, but her eyes seemed too deep to notice Fitz or Zack. She was likely thinking about home. Maybe she was thinking about her family, too. The next morning, Damon decided to tackle the subject up front.

He approached Fitz at the breakfast bar in the miner's cafeteria. Zoe wasn't up yet. Zack was out getting lost...somewhere safe.

"He is safe," Fitz said automatically. Again, he had forgotten his pact with Damon—no more telepathy. "Unless it were an emergency situation," he bluntly reminded.

"This isn't about Zack," Damon answered swiftly. "It's Zoe I'm scared for. She doesn't fit with us."

"Ah," said Fitz, "That is a matter that you may never discuss with Zack."

"Really?" said Damon, baffled. "What for? You mentioned this demon thing inside her when Zack was there in the portal room with me."

"Indeed," Fitz clipped. "Such is an error in judgment I must not afford to overlook again, my lord.

"You must understand: The Illori are no children's fable. They are their nightmares, as our emperor witnessed this eve."

Damon sucked up his juice. "But he said spiders and albino frogs."

"Indeed," said Fitz. "They are but intimate factors in an Illorul's sacrificial rite. I cannot yet explain this to you, as your mind is absent of the required education to life."

"Heh," said Damon. "Don't blame me for not knowing. Blame my culture."

They left it at that. It took an entire afternoon for Damon to realize that Fitz guided him off subject. He approached the worm dog after dinner to rectify the matter.

"Are we taking Zoe home before we move on?"

Fitz stared down at him, dumb-founded. He had been walking on only his hind legs for the bulk of the day, a stark opposite of him walking on all four. Damon himself noticed the lift in the moon's gravity as of late. He strode further with a lot less effort. That could be why he settled for half the blubber meat this time.

"Zoe?" He spoke like he'd never heard the name. Then his brows spiked up on alert. "Oh, the delicate one. I can never remember such a stark name."

"Same here," Damon noted. "Zack watches so much bossy mouse TV." Fitz didn't flinch for a moment.

"The delicate...Zoe has a matter of her own," he stated in almost a stutter. "I fear she requires far more attention than the two of you combined."

"You already mentioned this demon thing," Damon said, pausing for thought. "Hey, is that why we're collecting these?" He held out his stone before Fitz's staggering figure. The blue ember ebbed angrily in Fitz's eyes.

Fitz pushed Damon's hand back, gently. "Please hide that from me."

"Okay," Damon complied wearily. "But you are planning something with these stones, aren't you?"

"What makes you so certain?"

Damon frowned. What an odd question to throw.

"Uh..." He looked for the entry. "I think after all this stuff about Dad and how Dad—my Dad—had a stone when they...uh...turned into one guy, and..."

"When the host possessed your father's soul," Fitz stressed impatiently. "Yes, yes. I see your point. Quite frankly, I did not wish to involve myself in such a conversation. It is perhaps too painful to discuss."

Damon growled. This is getting nowhere.

"Are we taking Zoe back home or not?"

"No!" Fitz answered. "No, my lord. Zoe is not in the proper condition to return to her family. We still require eight stones to remove the Illorul from her body. We also require a proper location and the desired relic to ensure that the demonic purge does not involuntary kill the host."

Damon shed a tear. "You mean like Dad?"

Fitz nodded. "Whatever injury you've seen upon him mattered not of his condition."

"Then..." Damon paused. Now, his words ebbed away. "Then, I killed Dad?"

"The host, you mean." Fitz didn't mean his answer as a question.

Damon nodded. He must know.

"No," Fitz answered. "Your father remains alive and well. All your life, the actions of your host were purely of the soul trapped within the body. That is perhaps why he did not recognize you upon his final breath."

More tears. "Yes," Damon sniffed. "I guess you can..." He jerked his head away. Inside, his brain pinched his nerves, sending an arc of pain through his neck.

A hand snuck up on Damon's shoulder, the hand that pinned him down on his bedroom floor that fateful night. So many days have passed. It felt more like a year than half a month. So much had happened.

"Your grief catches up once in a blue moon," said Fitz. "It catches up with all intellectual beings in the Known Galaxy at one time or another." Those words haunted Damon all through the night.

Three days in.

Damon found himself with his first human meal for what felt like years: a garden vegetable omelet with quarter pound of bacon and a slice of lightly buttered toast. Surprisingly, Zoe proved herself a good bacon fryer, too. It did not feel too mushy, nor too charcoaled. It felt crisp and gentle all the way through.

Here, Fitz announced the discovery of a platoon vessel in one of the larger docking bays. He also mentioned a ship much similar to his own.

"It actually may be my own," he recalled. "I did once save the Earth from the Illori, correct, Lord Zack?"

Zack nodded his head too slowly. His mouth gummed down a good load of omelet and bacon. His stomach thanked him for the pleasure as his thoughts recycled themselves.

"It's about time," Zoe muttered next to Damon's ear. Damon bit into a piece of bacon and ignored her.

"So, which ship's the best for us?" he said, waving his fork in the air.

"Neither shall work for travel," Fitz answered coolly. "On a different note, I may safely address our requirement for proper nutrients and equipment on our exit within the incoming terran week. We should find an ample amount of these requirements on the platoon vessel, but not before we observe the interior of the smaller craft first."

Damon's eye twitched. Fitz isn't using his words properly here.

He was hiding something.

"I take it there's another portal room, then?" Damon suggested.

Fitz stiffened his eyes. "Please refer to them as..."

"Portal rooms," Damon answered, his face matching Fitz. "Technical terms aren't my thing, remember?"

"Indeed," said Fitz. "To answer your question: Yes, there are two more generators to be aware of..." A pause. "I thought I already mentioned them."

Damon grunted. "It must've slipped my brain." It didn't. Worrying about Mom and Zack turned to be his focus for the last little while. Not hearing her voice for so long left a bottomless pit in his heart.

Fitz blinked Damon's way. "Is there more curiosity that I should be concerned of?" Damon stared back, his mouth empty, yet damp. A sharp nudge to the gut turned his eyes to Zack. Zack gave him a ferocious scowl.

"He's asking if you have any questions, jerk!"

Not this again. Only when Damon felt absent of Zack's distasteful jabs did one hit him in the heart yet again. Like before, Damon pretended to ignore him.

"No questions," he said. "I need more time to think. That's all."

"Understandable," Fitz bowed. "But may I remind you? You have yet to question your father's whereabouts or of our first destination for that matter."

Damon nodded kindly. "I'll know when we get to the subject."

"On the contrary," Fitz noted, "you must attempt more study on your part if you wish to join in on our situation. To simply pass it off until the last possible moment—when we require your assistance the most—you would certainly falter."

Damon acknowledged with another nod. "I'm faltering as it is, thanks. Zack, you know more about our galaxy than I do. You can handle it, right?"

The brat gave him an abysmal stare. Damon tried breaking through, but something kept bouncing him back.

Damon stood before a massive pane of Poly-Flex glass, his mind reaching into the meeting. It happened nearly half a day ago, and yet it felt like he left the cafeteria for this spectacular view.

What a view it was, ever brighter than the view he had been used to for so long. No matter how many times he gazed out and watched the magnificent Earth loom ahead, it always brought a sense of wonder he felt only on his trip to Banff. Those were wonderful times, though. His family was there. Damon remembered the lookout photo all too well.

Here, he couldn't get that feeling. He stood here all alone, despite Fitz's occasional passes, despite Zack's constant harassment through the facility's com-link system.

Yet, he couldn't help but think about Zoe. Was he really as lonely as she was? Why didn't he go and ask?

Earth told him otherwise—the marvelous ball of blue, tan, and green, mixed with the ever-changing swirls of cloud cover. Here Damon stood, living a dream he'd never thought possible. He actually saw home from outer space. Yet for how long? Any moment now, Fitz would be calling them all to one of the remaining portal rooms. They would all jump through to the next place, and the next, too, if they couldn't find one of those stones—Elder stones.

It was like one of those kid's shows where a cocky brat goes around collecting monsters or rare treasures, one episode at a time. It'd take forever to get a decent collection, and then some to get out of those larger, more dangerous situations. Zack used to watch them side by side with Damon. Then, even Zack turned away, his focus more on beating bullies up at school.

Elder stones.

What was the point of collecting them again?

Damon drifted out of his shell. In the distance, well beyond the stars, Dad was hiding somewhere. Beyond that, Zack was meant to meet his so-called destiny. He....

A foghorn blared in Damon's ears. Amber lights drifted all over, forcing speed into his feet. He sped to the nearest stairs—a spiral set leading up to the tower bridge high above. This amber light…it was no drill.

Danger was afoot.

Fitz stood at center of the massive ball-shaped vault peaking the tower. His eyes were closed, feet fused to the oyster-speckled base floor. The rest of the room, all of it, carried as much sparkle. There were no breaks, no sign of the outside world.

Damon came in the usual and the only way in—through the gravity tube underneath their feet. He caught his breath and apologized at once. "One of the hatches shut on me before I could get here. I had to take the long way..."

Fitz interrupted with a finger of note. His voice crackled through the speakers in this solitary room. "A moment, please."

Damon didn't have the nerve to wait. Zack and Zoe hadn't made it to the dome yet. Fitz meant it as their rendezvous in case someone activated the warning protocol.

"Where...?" Damon began sharply.

"In a moment!" Fitz answered, his voice acting like a double-edged sword. Damon complied hesitantly. His fingers wouldn't stop fidgeting with one another.

The sickening amber light prodded the back of Damon's eyes. Its hypnotic strobe pierced his focus, skewered and crisped it atop a pyre. With all this silence flaking his lobes, he couldn't figure left from right, up from down. This blank room had done this to him before, though never with any lights blinking at his face.

His patience leaked out like sand in a broken hourglass. The less he carried in his heart, the more his body rattled in the deadly silence. Soon, he was going to break. Soon, he'd have no choice but to look for Zack.

Where were they?

A figure rose from the gravity tube. Zoe stepped into the amber light, her hair dripping wet. Her body was wrapped with either a massive fur towel or some kind of carpet creature Damon had yet to hear about."Okay," she sighed. "What's with the drill?"

"This isn't a drill," Damon answered. He placed his finger on his lips before she'd speak another word. "Where's Zack?"

Zoe shrugged like it didn't matter. Damon gave her a lip and a scowl.

Fitz stirred in a sudden lurch. "I have located the malfunction," he announced. "Rather troubling to locate, I must add. Whatever had set it off was deep in the electronic system." Damon could only grin.

"Aha!"

Damon stood erect. "Aha what?"

"Pest alarm in Sub-sector Gamma-Twelve. Artificially set, I fear." Fitz bared his amber eyes. "Not by Zack or either of you, I fear. Someone.... Hold the thought."

"What?" Damon blurted. "What, Fitz? Where's Zack?"

"You read my thoughts like a telepath," Fitz groaned. "Beyond that, however, the matter of our emperor has grown grave."

"Where is he?" Damon blasted.

Fitz twitched, eyes shut. For a moment, he simply stood in the floor, leaving Damon with nothing but blank heartbeats and crunching gasps. Then....

Fitz pulled his feet out of the floor. What was once liquid solidified like the surface was never disturbed.

The worm dog's eyes dawned on Damon almost at once. "He has left the facility!" Fitz exclaimed. "The alarm was meant to clear out the southern cone and the larger of the two docking bays."

"You mean the one with the platoon ship," Damon shot. "Yeah, I figured. But what's that got to do with...?" His head suddenly spun out of control. "Aw crap!"

"Indeed," Fitz nodded. "Your brother's shelter is situated in that very district. The nearest vessel he could board would have been the platoon vessel. And now, that vessel is undocking."

"Stop it!" Damon shouted. "Fitz, shut the doors or something."

"I cannot," said Fitz. "I have been forced out of the security system before I could intervene."

Damon lunged for the gravity tube. Fitz blocked him. "Out of my way!" Damon barked, slapping Fitz aside. His arm snagged on Fitz's wrist, twisting behind his back. He found himself against the oyster floor within seconds.

"You cannot intervene," Fitz explained sharply. "The security override prevents us from leaving this room until I can reconnect to its root structure."

"Let me go!" Damon howled. "This is my brother we're talking about! I'm not going to let him go again."

"You must!" Fitz snapped. "You must, Lord Damon. Otherwise..." Here Damon felt Fitz's restraints float freely away. "Otherwise," said the worm dog, "you shall succumb to its wrath. You do not wish to die young, my lord."

Damon limped to one leg. "But he's my brother!" he stomped. "He's my only brother...my last..."

He stopped right there. "Breathe, Damon!" He told himself repeatedly. "Breathe. Let Fitz handle this. He knows what's best for both of you."

Finally, he lifted his tear-swollen face. He looked Fitz in the eye and said, "Then what do we do?"

Continued...